Tombyards & Butterflies

By

Orlando A. Sanchez

A Montague & Strong
Detective Novel

I remembered my grandfather, my sister, and various aunts and cousins, in their coffins and gone forever in the tombyards where the butterflies settled like flowers on the graves and where the flowers blew away like butterflies over the stones.

-Ray Bradbury, *Zen in the Art of Writing.*

ONE

WHAT'S MORE EXCITING than chasing a rabid werewolf in the middle of the night? Chasing that rabid werewolf in Downtown Manhattan in the middle of the night. The Village, as a neighborhood, was a warren of intersecting streets and dead ends. We had already been at it for thirty minutes and we were closing in.

"This is what the English did," I said as we ran down Sixth Avenue. "Who lays out a city like this? A grid, Monty, would it have killed them to use a grid?"

"The Dutch were here first," he said. "The English didn't arrive until 1664. That's how you get the name New York."

We chased it down Minetta Lane off Sixth Avenue. The wet-dog smell punched me in the face as soon as I turned the corner.

"There's something wrong with that smell," I said. "God, he reeks!"

"I didn't realize you were a werewolf scent expert,"

Monty said as he caught up, his long legs making it easy.

"I'm not, but this guy smells like he hasn't bathed in a year. And did you see his eyes?"

"I did," Monty said. "He seems to be suffering from some kind of reaction."

"Reaction? He tore that poor woman in half. That's not a reaction. That's a full-blown infection."

"It does seem like he's unstable," Monty said as he looked up and down the street.

"Just a bit, yeah."

We followed the scent to the end of Minetta and on to Macdougal Street, when a large, furry blur shot past us.

"Shoot it, Simon! Shoot!"

"What do you think I'm doing?" I said as I fired several times.

"Shoot it harder!"

We jumped behind a parked SUV. The license plate read RUFFRDR. The truck was one of those huge things that wasn't quite a tank but could never pass for an ordinary car, either. I figured there was enough vehicle to protect us from the Were's razor-sharp claws. That theory evaporated, though. We jumped to the side as it sliced through the metal and plastic with ease, rendering our cover useless. The SUV fell apart like blocks of LEGO and I couldn't help thinking that RUFFRDR was going to wake up in the morning and have a very bad day.

"Really, that's what you're going with, Monty? 'Shoot it harder'?"

"Strong," rasped the creature on the other side of

what used to be a perfectly functioning mode of transportation. "I'm going to rip out your intestines and eat them while you watch."

"Wow," Monty said. "He's pissed. What did you do to him?"

"Now would be a good time for magic," I said. "You know, a fireball or two? Or some Were-melting spell?"

"Can't—he's wearing a null proximity rune," Monty said. "But I don't understand why the silver ammo isn't affecting him. You did switch out for silver ammo, right?"

"Silver…ammo? Of course I packed the silver—shit."

I forgot to switch the ammo.

"You forgot, didn't you?" Monty said, exasperated. "We're out here fighting a *werewolf*, Simon."

"I know," I said. "It's a little hard to miss."

"I'm going to die," he said as his voice hiked up an octave. "Out here on the filthy street, alongside you. Wonderful."

"No, I just misplaced it," I said with feigned indignation. "Hey, I had to pack all the bags while you did your meditation thing to charge the magic you're currently *not* using."

Monty narrowed his eyes and glared.

"Are you saying this is somehow *my* fault?"

"I'm just saying a little magic would make this go smoother, especially since I forgot to pack the silver ammo."

The werewolf shoved the debris of the SUV to one side. Saliva dripped from the corners of his mouth as he snarled loudly enough to rattle some of the windows. I jerked my head to one side to let Monty know that tall, dark, and fangy was about to shred us.

"Monty? Werewolf!!" I said, pointing at the large, angry creature closing on us.

Monty turned, opened his hands, and formed two large spheres of air in his palms. They were the size of basketballs and whirled with tremendous force, kicking up the detritus around us.

He let them go and they slammed into the werewolf, smashing it into the building across the street with enough force to dislodge a wheelbarrow full of bricks. The Were bounced off the wall and fell to the street face-first, unconscious. I holstered my gun, Grim Whisper, and ran over. The Grim Whisper was a custom designed and runed M&P Shield 9mm adapted to hold ten rounds plus one in the chamber. It had enough power to stop most supernatural threats, especially with modified ammo. For everything else, I had Monty.

I put a pair of silver restraints, individual bracers designed to prevent transformation, around his front legs, and he slowly morphed back to human. Now we stood over a naked man in the middle of the street.

"Did you bring the extra set of clothes?" Monty asked as he looked around and brushed the dust off his suit. He kept his shoulder-length hair loose and moved a few strands out of his face. His eyes gave off a subtle yellow glow, which happened every time he used magic.

I reached into my pack and pulled out a pair of jeans and a large T-shirt. It was one of my old 'I love New York' shirts, where the 'love' is replaced with a large red heart.

"I hope you know this shirt is a collector's item," I said as I dressed the Were. "You can't get them anymore."

"Unless you take a stroll around Times Square," Monty said and shook out his hands. "Hurry up, Simon."

"I thought you couldn't use magic on it?"

"I couldn't, I used magic *around* it."

I pulled out my phone and dialed the one number I knew would be working at this hour of the night.

"NYTF, Lieutenant Ramirez speaking," answered the voice.

Angel Ramirez had been with the NYTF for the last five years. He was rough around the edges, tough as hell, and a loyal— if not slightly crazy—friend. The only person I trusted more was Monty.

The New York Task Force, or NYTF, was a quasi-military police force created to deal with any supernatural event occurring in New York City. They're paid to deal with the things that can't be explained to the general public without causing mass hysteria.

"I want my dinner at Peter Luger's this weekend," I said. "On you."

"Simon, *el fuerte*, you got him?" Ramirez asked. "No way!"

"Of course I got him," I said as Monty scowled and raised an eyebrow at me. "Well, Monty got him, but I tracked him."

"Then maybe Monty should get Luger's, not you. I'm sending a bus over. Where are you?"

"Macdougal and Minetta."

"Is he silvered?" Ramirez asked. "Or are we walking

into a shitstorm?"

"We wouldn't be having this conversation if he weren't."

"Hang tight, they'll be there in ten."

I ended the call only to have my phone ring again. Santana's "Black Magic Woman" played and I seriously considered not picking up.

"Answer it," Monty said. "You know she'll just show up if you don't."

Bracing myself, I answered the call.

"Chi, what a surprise."

"You know I hate that name," she said. "Where are you?"

Actually, I did know. That's exactly why I always used it.

"I'm kind of in the middle—"

"Save it. Your office, twenty minutes," she said and hung up.

I looked at the phone for a few seconds before dropping it in my pocket.

"I think she's fond of you," Monty said with a smile. "Certainly sounds like it."

I gave him my best 'I'll stomp you silly' glare.

"What's wrong with your face?" he asked. "Are you injured, or constipated?"

"Hilarious." I waved him away. "You going to be okay here with Scooby?"

"Who?"

"The Were," I said, pointing. "The guy we just caught?"

"You're the one going to meet a vampire and you're asking me if I'm going to be okay?"

He had a point.

TWO

ON MY WAY to meet Chi at my office, I ran into my landlord.

Olga Gabriella Rodensky Etrechenko gave the term 'ice queen' a new meaning. Impeccably dressed, she always wore the latest in Italian or French haute couture. She stood in the lobby of my building, the Moscow, and peered down at me as if noticing an ant on her shoe. I walked past Andrei, the door attendant, who I think competed in strongman competitions in his spare time—(and if he didn't, he should).

Olga's thick accent and husky voice simultaneously aroused and terrified me. She fixed me with her glacial blue eyes and smiled. Her blond hair rested loose around her face and completed the Valkyrie look.

"Stronk," she said, never able to manage the 'g' at the end of my name. She beckoned with a finger.

"Hello, Olga," I said. "You're looking stunning, as usual."

"This old thing? Last year," she said, gesturing at her

dress that had probably cost enough to feed an entire Third World country. She pursed her lips and then locked eyes with me. "You owe last month."

I didn't know how she tracked me, but she always knew. In addition to being the resident ice goddess, she was also my landlord. If the rumors I heard were true, you never cheated Olga. My knees locked in place and my legs refused to listen. I took a deep breath and found my voice.

"I just finished a job. I'll have it by the end of the week."

"Good. Give envelope to Andrei by end of week," she said and walked out into a waiting Bugatti Veyron Sang Noir. She drove off and I found I could breathe normally again. I let out a long breath and Andrei gave me a smile and short nod. Being around her was like looking at the sun—great in short doses, lethal in the long term.

My office/home was located in a converted loft space on 14th Street and 11th Avenue in what used to be the Vault, an old BDSM club, but was now the property of one Mrs. Etrechenko. I never saw her husband. I assumed she had just eaten him on the night of the wedding and then carried on with life.

I was on the second floor and I used the stairs. The building itself used to be an old factory before it was a BDSM club and then converted to loft spaces. I shared the floor with Christye, Blahq, and Doil—a law firm of questionable character that occupied three quarters of the floor. They were closed as usual. I kept to a night schedule, which meant I rarely saw any of them, but I would hear of their exploits in the news. Occasionally they would refer a client my way, probably out of pity.

I briefly removed a smudge from our silver plaque, which read Montague & Strong Investigators and was located to the left of our door. I still think it should've said Strong & Montague, but Monty suggested that S&M Investigators would bring us a 'whips, chains, and cuffs' type of clientele. He bought the plaque and put up most of the seed capital, so I figured I'd let him have his way.

I opened the thick stainless steel door and disabled the state-of-the-art alarm system, which I was assured was so sensitive it could pick up a fly farting as it flew by. I walked past our small reception area and office. I made my way to the living area that sat behind another door at the rear of the space.

In the middle of my living room sat Michiko, or Chi as I called her. So much for my ultra-sensitive alarm. Michiko Nakatomi belonged to one of the most ancient vampire clans on the planet. When feudal lords were fighting over parcels of land, her family owned entire islands. Her family also helped form the Dark Council, the ruling body of supernatural beings that governed all supernatural activity.

Tiny, she barely topped five feet, and looked more like a character out of an anime with her long black hair than the force of lethality I knew and loved. She sat motionless in a red blouse and black business pantsuit.

Her emotionless black eyes followed me as I entered. I removed my shoes, a habit I learned from my sensei, and went to the kitchen to prepare some green tea.

In the distant past, she was known as *Karitori-fu*—the

reaping wind. Tales of her exploits became legends. I
was pretty sure they still used stories of her in Japan to
make children behave.

I brought over two *yunomi*, Japanese tea cups that I
kept for her infrequent visits, and served her tea first.
We sat at a *chabudai*, a low table designed for these
kinds of occasions. She nodded and took her cup,
savoring the aroma of the tea for a few seconds before
taking a sip.

"I have a situation," she said in her clipped English.

"Human?" I asked.

She took another sip and shook her head.

"Why not have the Dark Council handle it? You sit
on the governing body."

"The Council can be a bit heavy-handed and I need
a lighter touch—an outsider's touch, like yours,"

I was about as subtle as a brick thrown through a
window. The flattery was setting off all kinds of
alarms.

"So you need plausible deniability," I said. "How bad
is it?"

"It has to do with a shunned vampire from another
clan."

I raised my eyebrow at her and slowly set my cup on
the table. Vampires rarely got involved in other clans'
affairs. It led to miscommunications and usually a few
messy deaths.

"And you can't be seen to be involved," I said.
"What did this vampire do?"

"It's complicated. I just need you to collect her
before the Council does."

"Collect? A vampire?" I asked. "What am I

supposed to do with this vampire when I do?"

"Keep her safe," she said. "She will be at this address later tonight." She handed me a photo and a slip of paper with an address written in a neat and meticulous way. I recognized her handwriting immediately. "She won't be in your care for more than a night."

I looked at the picture and saw the image of a young woman in her late twenties. She was above average-looking, but nothing too remarkable. The one thing that stood out was the woman's red hair.

"How old is she and what's her name?" I asked. Pointing at the picture, "Is that her real color?"

It helped to have some of the pertinent details before taking on suicide missions. Redheads were rare enough; red-headed vampires were almost non-existent. Something to do with the genes during the turning. It meant this woman had the potential to become a powerful vampire, if she lived long enough. The shunning made sense now.

"She's still young, around five years old, and her name is Georgianna Wittenbraden—yes, from those Wittenbradens," she said when I made a face. "Be at that address in two hours and make sure you collect her…alive. Take the mage with you."

"Tristan? Really?"

"Yes," she said and raised her cup to her lips. She drank while boring into me with her dark eyes. "Unless you happen to have another mage hidden around here somewhere, yes, him."

"Should I expect a Council hit squad there?"

"No one calls them that anymore. The Council calls them Resolution Teams now. And no—she should be alone."

"This would be much easier if I didn't have to bring her in alive. Dead vampires don't fight back," I said, shifting my weight as my legs started to fall asleep.

"She'll be hungry, which will require precaution on your part. She's young, but she's formidable."

"The best precaution would be blasting her with UV lights and then picking up the charbroiled remains."

"Not an option," she answered and delicately placed the cup on the table and stood effortlessly and bowed. "*Arigatou gozaimasu*, thank you for the tea."

I tried to stand gracefully, and failed. "*Kochira koso arigatou gozaimasu*, thank you for the visit, it was my honor, Michiko," I said and bowed in response after regaining my balance.

"I am pleased to hear that your Nihongo is improving," she said with a brief smile. "There will be compensation once she's in your custody. Her parents would like her...relocated."

"And you're facilitating the relocation," I said, finally understanding her role. "What's your connection to her?"

She gave me a cold stare and my next question evaporated. Sometimes I forgot she was a deadly agent of destruction, capable of violence in a split second.

"There's no connection as far as she's concerned and I want it to remain that way," she said after a pause.

"So what do I tell her when she asks? She will ask. At least, I would."

"I don't care how you explain your presence there," she replied in her clipped tone. "Convince her you're not there to kill her, and keep her alive."

"Got it," I said with a nod and a shrug of my shoulders. "Have a rational conversation with a hungry vampire who doesn't know me. Should be easy."

"If this were easy, I wouldn't be here. Failure will cause my…displeasure."

"I'll get it done. She'll either be here by morning, or we'll have been horribly mauled."

"Simon, I can't stress enough how delicate a matter this is," she said and walked up to me. Even in heels, she only came up to my chest. Her long black hair framed her face as she looked up at me, and my heart paused for a millisecond. "If you screw this up, if the Dark Council needs to get involved, I'll kill you slowly with my bare hands."

I smiled.

"Chi—I've been forty for the last five years."

She smiled back and my blood froze in my veins.

"It seems your recent entry into immortality has given you a slight case of SOSS," she said and patted my chest lightly. "It's okay. I've seen these symptoms before in our newly turned vampires. It never lasts long, and neither do they."

"SOSS? What's SOSS?"

"Sudden onset supernatural stupidity. New vampires think that because they've become immortal, they can't die."

"But they can," I said, remembering a few vampires I turned to ash. "Vampires are immortal unless destroyed."

"My point exactly," she said and disappeared.

THREE

I CHECKED THE photo again and called Monty. He picked up on the second ring.

"What?" he said, annoyed.

"Did they pick him up?" I asked, turning the photo in my hand.

The NYTF was usually good with these sorts of things, and Ramirez was solid, but I also had Olga to worry about so I wanted to make sure.

"You saw Olga, or rather she saw you," he said.

I could hear the smile. "Yeah, I told her the end of the week."

"You have the most fascinating women in your life, Simon."

"That's me, the most interesting man in the world. Did Ramirez make the payment?"

"He did and he also said to forget Luger's since I did most of the heavy lifting and you were basically a tour guide."

"Bastard," I said with a laugh. "He could've at least

offered to take you."

"He knows I don't eat meat. He was being gracious in not offering."

"Luger's has some great salads, I'm sure."

"You're stalling. What did your vampire want?"

"It's a job—under the radar," I answered after a pause. "No DC."

"Wonderful. Is this a *paying* job? Or are we doing more charity work?"

"She said we would be compensated."

"Compensation for a vampire isn't what you imagine."

"Sounded like the financial kind," I said.

"Did you get that part in writing or did she just bat her eyes at you and stop your heart? Seriously, I don't see the attraction."

"Well, she's—" I started.

"I was talking about *her*. Tell me about this job and why under the radar?"

I explained the details and gave him the address. I stressed that she'd said to bring him along.

"200 Park Avenue. And we need to *collect* this Wittenbraden vampire alive? It's a trap—decline."

"I can't, it's Chi. What's the issue? I'm sure the two of us can handle a five-year-old vamp."

"You don't recognize the address?"

"I do, the MetLife building, the one that bisects Park Avenue."

"Yes, and also the home to the MetLife Donor Center—a blood bank."

"A vampire at a blood bank? That makes no sense. Is she planning a withdrawal?"

"Here's something else that doesn't make sense," he said. "How does *your* vampire know she will be there in two hours?"

"She wouldn't unless she—shit, this *is* a setup."

"Precisely, so walk away."

"They're going to kill her at the blood bank. That's why Chi can't be part of this. She wants us to stop them."

"If the girl's been shunned, why go through this elaborate production? There's something else going on here."

"I'll pack the bag and meet you at Roselli's."

"UV lights and silver ammo. Make sure you bring them, especially the ammo, *this time*," he said.

I winced at the mention of silver ammo. "Got it, putting it in the bag now."

I grabbed a few magazines of specially coated silver ammo for the Grim Whisper and tossed them into my Mach 3 backpack. This silver wouldn't kill them like it did the Were, but it hurt like hell. They cost a small fortune but had saved my life on more than one occasion.

"Ramirez said something I need to look into. It may be nothing, but it sounded off. I have to go to the morgue," Monty said, sounding distracted.

"The morgue? You need me to come along?"

"No, this is just a routine ID. I'll meet you at Roselli's in forty-five minutes. Get my usual."

Roselli's meant I would have to upgrade what I was wearing or else suffer the owner's ridicule.

FOUR

GRAND CENTRAL TERMINAL at night was a wonder to behold, if you slowed down long enough to take it in, that is. Roselli's catered to the 'night crowd,' as they referred to the supernatural community, by making the after-midnight menu exorbitant, even by New York City standards.

This didn't stop some of the more adventurous and wealthy New Yorkers from dining in the exclusive restaurant, where a filet mignon could set you back upward of two hundred dollars. They didn't realize, though, that if they weren't careful, some of the clientele would consider *them* part of the menu.

The owner, Piero Roselli, was a vampire from the old country. He'd never told me which part of the old country, except to say that it was far away. He was an older-looking man with a dignified air. I always joked that he was the original most interesting man in the world. He could always be seen wearing a dark suit with an indigo shirt. He never wore a tie.

"Tell me why I would put a *laccio*…a noose around my neck?" he once asked me. It didn't stop him from being my fashion critic.

A few years back, Monty and I had sat in Roselli's and I told him wearing a suit made it difficult on the cases I worked. He made a tsking sound and grabbed my cheek hard, and explained it to me.

"You look at this one—the spy, he's English, what's his name…Bond?"

"That's a character from a movie, Piero," I said, wincing as he squeezed my cheek.

"No," he said, and wagged his finger at me. "That is an idea. He fights, drives and makes explosions—in suit."

"If I did that, my suits would have to be made out of steel or Kevlar—*incomodo*, uncomfortable."

"Don't be *denso,* best material for suit is wool," he said and patted my cheek hard enough for me to see stars. "I call my tailor, Vincenzo from Chiaia in Napoli. You see him, and he makes some suits for you."

"Really, Piero, that's very gracious of you, but I don't think—" I started. Monty shook his head slightly, and I sighed. "Fine, I'll see your tailor."

"Good," he said with the matter settled. Then he pointed at me. "But no ties, eh?"

"No ties," I replied in an effort to avoid another seismic face-pat.

That was how I came to own a dozen handmade Neapolitan suits.

I walked into Roselli's and the crowd was just hitting its stride. Piero had expanded the restaurant a few years ago and added a dance floor one level down. I could hear and feel the bass beats reverberate through the floor and thump in my chest. The restaurant proper was two levels up.

As I ascended the steps, I could see a few members of the Dark Council occupying some of the more coveted tables. When I reached the highest floor, Piero glided up to me and stopped a few feet away. He sat everyone. If he didn't seat you, you weren't staying.

"Buona sera," he said and stood back to inspect my suit. After a few seconds, I got the almost imperceptible Roselli nod of approval. "Where is Montague?" He pronounced it "Montagooeh" and refused to be corrected.

"Evening, Piero," I said, distracted as I took a subtle headcount of Council members. "He said he'll be here soon. Looks like a full house."

"Simon," he said and grabbed me by the elbow as he led me to our table. He always pronounced the first syllable as 'see' instead of the traditional 'sigh,' "You work tonight?"

I nodded as I let my eyes scan the room. "I may have something to do a little later on, why?"

"*Consiglio Nero*," he said and pointed a finger at me, getting my attention. "Don't look, don't talk, eh?"

Apparently I wasn't as subtle as I thought. He stared at me until I nodded and then sat me down with my back to the rest of the room. Monty arrived ten minutes later with Piero shadowing him.

"Food or only business?"

"Both—I'm starving," I said. "The usual for Monty."

He nodded and left us alone. I slid the picture of Georgianna across the table. Monty took it and put it aside.

"That's from Ramirez," he said, passing me an envelope full of large bills. "It feels a little crowded for this time of night."

"I noticed. Could you do your thing?" I said and waved my hand around. "You know, the mute-button spell?"

"One moment," he said and shook out his hands. "It's not as easy as it looks, and it's not called the 'mute-button' spell."

"It should be."

He gave me a look and made a gesture with his hand. The sounds of the room became instantly muffled. Several of the patrons looked in our direction. Monty had effectively prevented them from overhearing our conversation. I also liked to call it his 'sphere of silence,' which he also hated, of course.

"She looks young," he said as he picked up the photo and looked at it. "Did your vampire give you a reason for the shunning?"

"No, and what are *they* doing here? I've never seen Roselli's this full of DC before."

"The same thing your vampire is doing, only a little more overt," he answered as he scanned around the room. "There's no way they could be involved with a vampire killing. They were having dinner here."

I checked my watch. We had an hour left before they planned to kill Georgianna.

"I still don't get how Chi knows she'll be there at that exact time. How can she be so accurate without setting it up?"

"I think I may have the answer to that one," he said

as Piero returned to oversee the placement of our plates. If he noticed that Monty had cast his sphere, he gave no indication and made sure the servers placed the plates just as he indicated.

Once everything was served, he gave us a short bow and stepped away. A large carafe of the finest distilled water on the planet would be our beverage for the meal. Monty had a large salad that I'm sure was picked from the richest soil in creation. I had a Japanese A5 wagyu filet. Roselli's was one of the few places in the city certified to serve authentic wagyu Kobe, and it showed.

We never ordered from a menu at Roselli's. He just appeared with what he thought I should have that evening along with Monty's usual. He hadn't been wrong yet.

"You were saying?" I said after stuffing a forkful of beef in my mouth. Monty just stared at me for a few seconds and chewed on his salad. We had put our dietary differences to rest long ago, but it never ceased to amaze him how much I ate.

"Why do you even bother?" he asked, looking at me with mild amazement. "It's not like you *need* to eat."

"Because I get hungry?" I said around another forkful. "Being immortal doesn't mean I don't get hungry."

"That's a double negative," he said. "'Being immortal doesn't stop me from desiring food' is more appropriate."

"Right now I desire this large slab of juicy beef," I said and cut another piece. "Being immortal has not killed my appetite."

"It should. You don't need food or much sleep and your body heals at an accelerated rate," he said as he gestured at me with his fork. "Magic-based attacks are useless against you. You're a perfect candidate for the mage school."

"Except I don't practice or trust magic," I answered. "Now, if you could get me a set of adamantium claws, I could"—I made a fist in front of my face—"*snikt* be a total badass."

He looked at me and groaned.

"No, please," he said, shaking his head. "We don't have time for your Wolverine fixation."

"Wolverine is the patron saint of badassery," I said, while nodding solemnly. "As such, Saint Wolverine can never be mocked—ever."

"Spare me. You should really consider apprenticeship at the Circle."

"Is this the same Golden Circle you're currently AWOL from?"

He narrowed his eyes and coughed into his hand. "That's different. I think they could help you."

"Don't need that kind of help, but thanks. Why don't you teach me? Aren't you one of the most powerful mages in the sect?"

"No," he said clenching his jaw. "I won't do that again."

I knew better than to prod. We had discussed this topic before and it never ended well.

"We have time for dessert?" I asked, changing to a less volatile topic.

"No, we have thirty minutes," he answered and finished his salad. "As I was saying, I think I know how your vampire figured out the hour."

"Less traffic?"

"Something like that," he said and placed his napkin on the table. " I did some checking and found out that the MetLife Donor Center gets several deliveries throughout the day, but because of its location, it receives the largest shipment in"—he looked at his watch—"about twenty-five minutes."

"Perfect target to hijack if you're a hungry vampire that, what—has poor social skills?" I said. "I don't buy it. She can take anyone off the street—she doesn't need to hit a bank."

"We may have a bigger a problem. My trip to the morgue was...disturbing."

"When is visiting a large group of corpses not disturbing?" "How's Allen?"

"According to him, one of his specimens disappeared."

"What do you mean—disappeared? Undead?"

"No, he said there was no trail and no decomposition," Monty replied. "A dead person just got up and walked out of the morgue."

"Dead people, with the exception of that group over there," I said, gesturing to the Dark Council vampires around one of the tables, "don't get up and leave the morgue of their own volition. He must've been mistaken and someone went zombie on him."

"We can look into it later, but right now we have to leave," he said, straightening his sleeves.

"Look into it later? Really?" I said, with a shudder. "I hate dealing with zombies. It's never like the TV show."

"Nothing is," he said and made another gesture, removing the sphere of silence. The sounds of the room rushed back at us, increasing in volume. "You need to excuse yourself or Piero will never forgive us."

As we stood, Piero appeared. I explained that we needed to leave and that we would have to miss the *dolce,* the dessert. Roselli's desserts redefined the concept of culinary genius. He shook his head and scowled, saying something unintelligible. Not having dessert with a meal was a serious breach of etiquette with Piero.

"I will have Giuseppe save you a piece of the Tiramisu Trece Negro," he said softly as he clasped his hands reverently, with a solemn expression.

His words impaled me where I stood. My eyes pleaded with Monty. "The Tiramisu Thirteen?" I asked, stunned.

"No time," Monty said, shaking his head. "Sorry, we can get some afterwards."

"You understand this is tiramisu with Remy Martin Louis XIII Black Pearl used as the cognac ingredient?"

"We...have...no...time," Monty stressed, pointing at his watch. "Let's go."

"Piero, please express my extreme disappointment to Giuseppe at not being able to enjoy dessert," I said, trying to sound contrite as I shot Monty a glare. "I'll come back to enjoy the magnificence of his craftsmanship."

Piero apparently sufficiently mollified with my grief gave us a short nod as we approached the stairs.

"Seems your vampire needed an alibi as well," Monty

said as we headed downstairs. He looked past me into the back of the room.

I scanned the back tables, and there, sitting next to several members of the governing body, was Michiko. She wore a form-fitting black silk dress with red accents. She didn't look my way, but I knew she saw me.

"Let's go," I said. My foul mood at missing dessert only became worse after seeing her seated at a table full of bloodthirsty killers. "I don't have time for her shit."

Her eyes narrowed slightly and I knew she heard me. I walked out, stood in front of Roselli's, and took in the cool night air. Monty stood next to me and exhaled.

200 Park Avenue was two blocks away. I checked the time. We would be fifteen minutes early. I turned down the block and started walking to the MetLife building.

"Angering her isn't very wise," he said as he kept pace next to me. "Despite your feelings."

"Do you realize Giuseppe makes that tiramisu, only two or maybe three times a year?" I asked. "What we just did, leaving without tasting it, should be considered a crime."

"Let me get this straight; the tiramisu, not your vampire, is the source of your irritation right now?" he asked in disbelief. "Did you pack the ammo?"

I nodded and handed him one of the Britenite B3a UV lights. About two feet long, B3's were long black cylinders of titanium and heavy enough to double as truncheons. They were powerful enough to stun most vampires without killing them.

"Not much time for recon. How do you want to play this?"

"We'll have to go up through the hotel and into the building proper," he said, putting the UV light in a pocket. "The delivery will be by armored truck in the rear. We should be there when it arrives."

"How do you know all of this?" I asked, surprised. "It's not like you're keeping tabs on the blood banks in the city."

"The Dark Council is comprised of roughly twenty-five percent vampires. Keeping track of blood sources in the city is a prudent strategy."

"You're keeping tabs on blood banks?" I said while strapping on my thigh sheath.

"Only the deliveries. It's good information to have, and knowledge is power."

"I need to get you a hobby," I said, shaking my head. "Let's go save a vampire."

FIVE

NOTHING SCREAMED DARK Council hit squad louder than a bunch of people trying to act casually invisible. 200 Park Avenue had several entrances. We entered through the hotel lobby to blend in and make our way to the service entrance without being seen. Monty and I stopped in the crowded lobby and looked around. It bustled with activity except for the pockets of men in corners wearing dark suits. I counted ten broken up in pairs around the room.

"They may as well be holding signs that say 'proud member of the Dark Council hit squad,'" I whispered to Monty as we made our way to the elevators.

"This group isn't the Resolution Team; they're here to prevent escape," Monty said as the door opened and we stepped in. "Every entrance will have a similar group."

"Isn't that overkill?" I asked.

He shot me a look. "Are you serious? They're vampires."

"But isn't that a bit much for one five-year-old vampire? How dangerous can she be?"

He pressed the button that would take us to the basement level. As the doors began to shut, two of the hit squad slid into the elevator and stood in front of us. The doors slid closed. As the car descended, I noticed they didn't press a button.

"What floor can I get you?" I asked as I held my hand over the panel.

The guy on the left moved, but I was ready. He shifted to the side and I hit him with a blast of UV light. Vampires are fast—faster than I can track—but in a small elevator, there are only so many choices. The light stunned him for a few seconds while Monty set his clothes on fire. The vampire on the right opted for a more professional touch and pulled a gun. I swung the light around, forcing him to duck and miss as he fired twice.

Monty slammed them with air and tried to force them against the sides of the elevator. It didn't work and the charbroiled vampire took a swing at me. I didn't dare use my gun—vamps were too fast, and I might shoot Monty. So I did the next best thing and jumped on him.

The fires had gone out, thanks to Monty using air, but the smell of burned flesh filled the elevator. The recently cooked vampire grabbed me by the throat and shoved me against the elevator wall. I tried to speak but my vision was tunneling in and I saw spots dancing. Michiko's words floated back to me about being immortal and still dying. I pulled my gun and emptied the magazine into the vampire. He smiled at me and began choking me harder.

"Monty, do it," I croaked. "Do it, now."

He nodded and made a quick gesture. "Sorry about your suit."

White-hot flames engulfed the elevator car, vaporizing the vampires where they stood. Monty had been holding back for fear of hurting me. The flames singed me, burning holes in my suit. My face felt tender, like after spending an afternoon at the beach, but I was unharmed. The itchiness let me know that it started healing immediately.

"Thank you for not incinerating me," I said, feeling my throat. "I don't like wizards or any magic-users, really. They're usually arrogant egomaniacs handling powers they barely understand. But you, Monty, I like, for some reason."

"Probably because I refrain from reducing you to ash where you stand. Like these two."

"Probably. Why would they attack?"

"They must have recognized us from Roselli's, or were given instructions to remove us once we arrived at the hotel."

"By whom?"

"That's a good question," Monty said as he looked through the ash and found the medallions. Each vampire carried a medallion signifying his or her clan. They were about the size of a quarter and made of copper. "I don't recognize this crest."

"That's not Michiko's clan," I said, relieved. "What clan is that? I've never seen it."

"It's not one of the European clans either," Monty said and pocketed the medallions. "And it's not a real hit squad. Their medallions are blank. That would explain the incompetence in the elevator."

"This is personal. Whoever is going after this vampire is settling a personal grudge."

"Yes, but with the approval of the Dark Council."

"Or at least its permission," I said.

"There's something deeper happening here or your vampire wouldn't have sent us. We'd better move quickly before it goes bollocks up."

Hit squads came in three flavors: the 'smother them with pain and death' variety that is a mob of dangerous but not too organized individuals. These were usually followed by the 'I'm a total badass' variety where the Council sends one or at most two elite total badasses to fulfill the contract.

My least favorite was the coordinated badass team, which was usually a three-to-five-member elite unit that worked seamlessly with the height of lethality and efficiency. Thankfully, we were facing the first option. The pros: they were going to be easy to dispatch. The cons: there was going to be a shit-ton of them to deal with.

"Silver ammo did jack to that vampire," I said, holstering my gun as the elevator doors opened. "I might as well be using rubber bullets."

We stepped off the elevator and headed to building's the rear garage.

"I noticed. Why didn't you use your mark or activate the runes on the gun?" he said, looking at my hand.

"Because I hate it, you know that, and it usually calls *her.*"

"Stop being so dramatic. I doubt she'll appear every

time you use it. She *is* busy, you know. Maintaining balance and all that," he said, waving a hand.

"The mark is for those moments when you stop and take stock of your situation and the only response is: 'we're fucked.' Besides, I figured you had this one."

"Your use of the mark doesn't encourage her appearing," he said. "That's just your superstition."

"Three out of three. She showed up the last three times I had to use it."

"Could be she's just interested in you. More likely she's bored and likes talking to you. She may be the only entity in existence who understands the inner workings of that thing you call a mind."

"That's hilarious. You've never had to speak with her."

"And I hope I never will." We rounded a corner and saw the signs that directed us to the loading dock and deliveries. "I don't intend to end up bloody daft—I have you for that."

We made our way to the loading dock, which was situated at the rear of the building. I peeked around one of the pillars. Around the dock, I saw more vampires hovering around the entrance to the building. They were moving into position. Some of them were dressed like office personnel and maintenance workers.

"You think they're waiting for the delivery?" I whispered.

Monty shook his head. "More likely what it will attract," he answered and pointed. "Delivery arriving."

A large truck could be heard some distance off and getting closer. The headlights shone down the ramp as an armored truck came into view.

"They deliver blood in that?"

He nodded and unbuttoned his jacket. "Secure transport deters from thefts en route. To vampires, blood is worth more than money. So it makes sense to ship it this way."

The truck pulled into the loading bay, opened its rear doors and all hell broke loose.

SIX

A BLUR SHOT past us as the doors opened. Then I saw Georgianna. She stood about up to my shoulder and looked like her picture except more on the feral side. Her eyes had gone vamp, which meant her pupils had expanded to cover the irises. It was probably to capture as much light as possible during hunting. I noticed her red hair leaned more to the orange end of the spectrum.

One of the hit squad closed on her and she ducked under the attack and raked her claws through his midsection, bisecting him. He fell in two parts as she jumped back from two more of the hit squad when they drew their short swords. She snarled as they closed on her.

"There's too many. She can't avoid all of them," I said, leaning around a column.

"She's quite impressive considering she's unarmed," Monty said.

"I wouldn't consider those claws unarmed. They're

almost Wolverine-worthy."

"Don't start. Maybe we can just wait until she thins the herd?" he answered, as the air around him grew warm.

"If they hurt her or worse, I'll let Chi know you wanted to wait," I said as I checked the Grim Whisper. "I'm sure she'll think it was a great strategy."

"Bloody hell, fine, let's crash the party."

"You ready? Once I say hello, they'll bump us to the top of the victim list."

Two fireballs formed in his hands and he nodded. I stepped around the column and began firing. Silver ammo didn't kill vampires, but it slowed them down. The upside of using silver was that it took a long time for them to heal from the wounds. The downside—it really pissed them off.

Fireballs sailed past my head as I ran to another pillar for cover. I looked at Monty and he just grimaced and motioned behind me. I turned in time to see two vampires close on me. I dodged a short sword aimed for my midsection, while the second tried to make me shorter by removing my head. I shot them both and blasted the UV light as they writhed on the floor in pain. Monty reduced them to ash as I closed on the armored truck and the target of the attack.

"The Grim Whisper is useless, it seems," Monty said as he joined me. "Use the soul."

I reached for the blade attached to my thigh but hesitated.

"Can't you just barbecue them all? It would be much easier than using this."

"My flames aren't sentient, Simon. I'll catch her too

and then you can have *that* conversation with your vampire about why you didn't want to use the one weapon designed for fighting supernatural beings."

"Fuck," I growled, and pulled out the blade. "This is going to suck."

The black blade seemed to absorb all the available light. Some of the hit squad hissed as they saw it, while others cursed under their breath. Michiko had given me the Ebonsoul when she discovered I was immortal. Something about walking outside of time and it being appropriate. Her family had held the blade for thousands of years. She gave it to me for safekeeping and to scare the shit out of the remaining clans.

Its real name, known only to Chi and myself, was *kokutan no tamashi*, which literally meant the ebony soul. I preferred the Ebonsoul because it was less of a mouthful. Its black blade was eighteen inches long and covered in ancient runes, of which Monty was only able to decipher half.

It was created to fight beings 'not of this world,' was the best he could tell me after weeks of study. I only knew it was effective against any supernatural being I came across. I hated it. If I used it too often, I could lose myself in a haze of bloodlust, which made me worse than the things I was fighting.

A hit squad member pounced, and I stabbed, ignoring the searing pain in my arm as he dug his claws into me. The Ebonsoul siphoned its lifeforce and fed it to me.

I made my way through the hit squad slashing and cutting those Monty left intact. With each kill, I grew stronger, faster, and less human. By the time we reached the truck, I was almost as feral as Georgianna. I rushed into a group of three and slashed through them before they could react. Their lifeforce coursed through my body. I turned to face the remaining hit squad members, but they were gone. We were alone with Georgianna. I stared at the red-haired vampire in front of me for several seconds before the voice registered.

"Simon, Simon, come back."

I heard the voice and a part of my brain recognized it. I kept my focus on the vampire in front of me, making sure she wouldn't move. Motion from the corner of my eye caught my attention and I whirled on it. A man was talking to me, but I didn't or couldn't understand.

"It's me—Monty. Put the sword away. It's done," he said with his hands up.

"Monty?" I said as I regained clarity. "What the fu —?"

Georgianna jumped on me and knocked the Ebonsoul from my hand as we tumbled to the floor. I looked up, dazed, and saw her about to rake my neck with her razor-sharp claws. A sphere of air punched into her and knocked her back into the wall. I scrambled to where the Ebonsoul lay and sheathed it. The effects of its siphon began to wear off.

"Monty! Don't kill her," I yelled as I approached her. "She's not in her right mind. Georgianna, Georgianna, we aren't going to hurt you."

She snarled at me.

"She needs to feed," Monty said and looked at the truck. "Keep her busy for a second."

"How do you suggest I do that?" I asked as she shook her head. "She doesn't seem open to meaningful conversation right now."

Monty jumped into the back of the armored truck.

"I know why she's here," his voice echoed from inside the truck. "Bloody hell, this *was* a trap."

"What gave it away?" I asked as I stepped back from the now focused Georgianna. "The ambush or the elevator welcoming committee?"

"Almost there," he said. "Just need to bring this to body temperature."

"Great, but you want to come out here before I need to use the blade? I don't think the UV light will do anything except make her angrier."

He leaped out of the truck with a blood transit container. A coppery smell filled the air as he tossed the container to Georgianna, who proceeded to drink the contents, not caring about spilling them over her face and clothing. She moaned with pleasure as she drank.

"She seems to be enjoying it and calming down. Like a good cup of tea."

"Tea?" I said, staring at him. "You clearly need help."

He was right, though. She had stopped snarling and her pupils were no longer dilated to the size of nickels. She leaned her head back against the wall, closed her eyes, and sighed.

"She should be regaining all her senses any moment now," he said as he picked up some of the blood containers.

"She sounds like you and your 'spot of tea' you go on about," I answered. "What's so special about this blood?"

"Collect as many of those containers as you can and get her out of here before more of that hit squad arrives," he ordered as he grabbed more containers and tossed them into a sack he found in the back of the truck. "The Dark Council is going to be displeased, which I think was your vampire's plan all along."

I followed his example and placed several of the containers in the hard pack. I slung it over my shoulder and approached Georgianna.

"How do you propose we get her out of here looking like that?" I asked, examining our blood drenched charge. "I'm sure the drivers of SuNaTran have seen worse, but she's literally a bloody mess."

"I have my car," she said with a slight accent I couldn't place. "Who are you?"

Monty and I both looked at her.

"I'll take the lorry and make sure they follow me," he said, moving quickly. "You take her to the Moscow and keep her safe."

"You'll take the *what*?" I asked with a smile. Monty usually slipped into his 'English' mode when stressed.

"I'll take the lor—truck, happy?" he said, exasperated. "Get her out of here."

"Where's your car? We need to leave before more of your friends come visit."

"They aren't my friends," she said with a trace of anger. "My car is up the ramp, but who are you? You aren't vampires."

"Right now we're the only reason you're still alive," I replied, looking around at the dead hit squad members. "You have a lot of enemies, even for a shunned vampire." I noticed she startled when I mentioned the shunning. No one outside a clan would know about it. "This many in a hit squad is angry with an extra dose of hate. Who did you piss off?"

"They're from my clan."

"Well, your clan sucks," I said closing my pack.

Monty jumped into the truck and started the engine. I ran up the ramp and saw a sleek blue Porsche Boxster S about halfway up. The license plate read GWB and I figured this was our ride. I gave her points for having the presence of mind to back it in. I stuck out my hand and she just stared at it.

"Keys," I said.

"To what?"

"Keys to the car so I can get us out of here. Before more unfriendliness arrives."

"You're not driving my car," she said as she walked to the driver's side. "Tell me where we're going."

She got in and revved the engine. I jumped in the passenger side, still in mild shock. "The Moscow on 14th and—"

"11th Avenue. I know it. Buckle up," she said, fastening her seatbelt.

I put my hand on the wheel and turned off the car.

"Let Monty get their attention or they'll follow us home. When you get out, don't drive like a maniac either."

Monty passed us in the truck and made a hard left at the entrance. Several hit squad members scrambled back to their waiting SUVs and gave chase. I counted three of the large black vehicles intent on stopping Monty. I almost felt sorry for them.

I took my hand off the wheel and she turned on the car again. It rumbled and purred to life. She was about to put it in gear when someone stepped into the middle of the ramp, blocking our path. She froze and gripped the wheel tightly enough to show the whites of her knuckles.

"Who—what is that?" she said, her voice trembling and her eyes locked on the figure in front of us.

"Turn off the car and stay inside," I whispered and moved slowly. "Whatever you see or hear, don't get out of the car. Understand?"

She nodded mutely as I stepped out. The car sputtered off and I gave her a brief nod of assurance. I made sure I had access to my mark and the Ebonsoul as I walked up the ramp.

Near the top of the ramp stood the Dark Council's version of a final response. It was Ken, Michiko's younger brother. He was impeccably dressed as usual, in what I liked to call 'sinister casual.' Sharing the same gene pool as Michiko meant he was lethally handsome, a trait he exploited with devastating resourcefulness. No one expects an assassin to be good-looking, and this one looked like a model.

"Hello, Ken," I said, letting my hand rest lightly on the sheath holding the Ebonsoul. My other hand rested lightly on my mark.

"*Konbanwa*, Simon," he said and gave me a short bow as he looked me over and smiled. "What's this look? Barbecue nouveau?"

"Monty is my fashion consultant, and I see you're still doing funeral festive. Are you on this hit squad?"

He wore a black trench coat over black jeans topped

by a black turtleneck sweater. I was seeing the trend. His long hair hung to his shoulders. The smile on his face never reached the dead eyes that looked through me. I shifted my hand to allow easier access to the Ebonsoul.

His eyes followed my hand movement and he laughed, which only made me more wary. He wore a katana across his back. It was rumored to be the sword, *kokutan no ken,* the pair to the Ebonsoul. I'd never seen it and didn't want to.

"Black is classic," he said with a smile that did nothing to ease the flip-flopping of my stomach. "If I were on this hit squad, we would be testing the limits of your so-called immortality right now."

I let out the breath I had been holding since the car stopped and took my hand off the hilt of the Ebonsoul.

"Why are you here, if it's not to remove body parts —not that I'm complaining."

"*Onee-san,* Michiko, requested my presence here, to observe and assist if needed."

"She what?" I said, surprised.

"I'm impressed. You didn't let the Ebonsoul consume you. Maybe she's right about you after all."

"This was a setup," I said, looking down the ramp at the carnage of the hit squad. "I just need to figure out who did the setting. Why are they after her?"

"Looks like her clan wants her dead."

"Yeah, I got that from the mob of angry vampires trying to end my life. Why do they want *her* dead? Isn't shunning enough?"

I looked back to the car and saw a petrified

Georgianna staring back at me, still strangling the steering wheel. I gave her a small smile and tried to let her know everything was okay.

"You need to ask the young lady that. I suggest you keep her safe, Simon," he said and adjusted the sword on his back.

"I'm working on it. It would help if they weren't trying to cut her to pieces."

"She's been shunned. Means it's a death sentence. What did you think would happen? They were going to have a *talk*?"

"Chi told me she would be here alone. This is the opposite of *alone*."

"I can't believe she still lets you call her that," he said, rubbing his chin. "Incredible. She can sometimes be vague on details, but she trusted you to handle this and it seems everything is in order."

"In order?" My voice rose a bit, as did his eyebrow. He cocked his head to one side and looked at me, amused. "Nothing is in order. I have this half-crazed vampire being attacked by a hit squad from a clan I've never heard of and now I'm transporting stolen blood. Does that sound in order?"

"Michiko would be displeased if something were to happen to her," he said and looked around. "You should leave now. More are coming. I'll be close and watching."

"Doesn't that make me feel all warm and tingly," I shot back, but he was moving fast.

He turned the corner and disappeared. I ran back to the car and jumped in. The engine purred to life.

"Who was that?" she asked as I sat in the passenger

side. "I couldn't move."

"Yeah, he has that effect on people. Listen, we can talk on the way. More of that hit squad is on the way and I don't want to be here when they arrive."

"I'm not half-crazed," she said, still choking the wheel in a death-grip.

"Who said you were?" I answered, looking behind us. "Can we get moving?"

"You did, when you were speaking to that creature. You called me half-crazed. Do I look half-crazed to you?"

I forgot about vampires and their heightened senses. I took a second to admire the tableau. She was gripping the wheel in a stranglehold. Her chin, neck, and the front of her shirt were covered in the blood she had gulped down earlier. It looked like she left "crazy" long ago, had rounded the corner, passed deranged and was heading into full-blown psycho any second.

"That *creature* is a vampire, just like you. I apologize for calling you half-crazed. What I meant to say was that staying here arguing about what I said while a hit squad is on its way is *completely* crazy."

"I'm not half-crazed, I was hungry," she whispered and loosened her grip on the steering wheel. "And he's nothing like any vampire I know."

"Fine, you were starving, not crazed. He's not like any vampire you'll *ever* meet, trust me. Can we go now?"

"Buckle up," she said with a tight smile.

Something in her tone made me check the seatbelt was secure. I clicked it into place and she gave me a sidelong glance.

"I'm ready," I said. "Remember what I said about driving like a—"

She stepped on the gas and screeched up the ramp.

I wasn't ready.

She set her jaw and shifted the gears. The next moment, my seat had been converted into a black hole, trying to suck me in as she sped out of the garage. All thoughts of conversation vanished as we hurtled onto Park Avenue. She headed up to 57th Street and then across town to the Westside Highway. Once on the highway, she raced downtown. I tried to look back several times to make sure we weren't being followed.

Considering our speed, I didn't think anything short of a Formula One racecar could keep up. I glanced over at the speedometer and saw the needle hovering near the red the whole time. I expected the flashing lights of the NYTF to appear any second. But if she was scared, it didn't show in her driving.

We pulled up to the Moscow and she stopped in front of the entrance.

"Never getting into a car with you, ever again," I said as I stumbled out the door.

Andrei didn't give me a second glance, but he took a few moments on Georgianna before opening the door. It's possible it had something to do with the fact that Georgianna looked like she had bathed in a vat of blood.

The valet slid silently into the car and took it to the underground parking garage as we entered the lobby. I lingered a moment and searched the inside pocket of my jacket.

"You in fire?" Andrei asked as he looked me up and

down, sniffing the air around me.

I felt the rumble of his bass voice in my chest. It sounded closer to an angry growl than an actual voice, especially with the accent.

"Something like that," I mumbled as I patted my pockets, found what I was looking for, and handed him the envelope of cash. "Tell Olga this month and next month."

"*Spasibo*," he said and put the envelope in a pocket.

Ramirez and the NYTF had come through sooner than usual, which meant I could breathe a little easier regarding Olga and the rent.

I never had an issue trusting Andrei—no one cheated Olga.

We headed upstairs and I noticed the door right away. It was slightly open and a light was on. I never left a light on. I pulled out my gun and motioned for Georgianna to wait behind me. She stood to one side as I approached the door. I pushed it open and found the office area empty.

"Stay here," I said as I poked my head back outside. "Let me check the back."

She leaned up against the wall, crossed her arms, and nodded. I headed to the living quarters and found Michiko standing in front of the large sofa in the center of the floor. Behind her, dwarfing the sofa, stood a giant.

"Really, Simon-*kun*, why don't you have your mage place some runic defenses on the property?" she said using an honorific meaning I was her junior. This was an official Dark Council visit or she was flexing her position for the giant's benefit. "The security system you currently possess, if you could call it that, is inadequate. This is why I brought Yama. Please come in, Georgianna."

I holstered the gun as Georgianna walked in behind me. If Andrei was a mountain, Yama was a mountain range. I couldn't imagine the vampire insane enough to try to turn him. So I figured he was human. A large human. Large enough to have his own gravitational field.

"Michiko-*sama*," I replied, using the honorific and bowing slightly. It didn't make sense to push it, especially in front of what she considered inferiors. If I called her Chi, she would probably rip off one of my arms just to make a point. "Why is there a rogue planet in my living room? And Tristan is not 'my mage,' he's my partner and friend."

She returned the bow and sat on the sofa. She wore black pants and a sleeveless black top. A red dragon imprint started at her left shoulder and wrapped itself around her, ending at her right hip. Her hair was pulled back into a tight bun, giving her the stern librarian look.

"Yama is here to make sure your charge is safe. We have a—complication."

I took a breath and kept my anger in check. Pissing her off would only get most of us hurt, dead, or both.

"You said it was only for one night," I answered, doing my best to keep my voice level. "You also said she was going to be alone. She wasn't."

"Ken tells me you resisted your weapon," she said with the hint of a smile. "I commend your spirit."

"My spirit, along with the rest of me, was nearly

shredded tonight by a hit squad."

"Yet here you stand, intact. Well done," she said with a short nod.

She was blowing smoke up my ass, which meant things were bad—as in catastrophic.

"*Arigatou gozaimasu*," I said, returning the nod, and never being one to rest on formality added, "So how screwed are we?"

Yama grunted and shifted forward, surprisingly fast for someone large enough to tilt the earth off its axis. I raised an eyebrow and smiled at him. He scowled back and narrowed his eyes. We were going to be best friends, I could just tell.

Michiko raised a hand and Yama froze in place. He said something in rapid Japanese and she answered just as fast. He bowed and moved back behind the sofa. My Japanese was rudimentary at best, but I caught something about him stomping on my head.

"He seems upset," I said, smiling at him.

"Yama believes you should be killed for your impudence. I informed him that aside from it being an impossible task, I forbid it."

That was when it happened. She showed up.

SEVEN

MOST PEOPLE CONSIDER karma to be an abstract concept. I knew her to be the mistress of bad-timing. The mark on my hand exploded with light and everything froze in place.

"Now? Really?" I looked around at everyone frozen in time. "This is *not* a good time."

A burning sensation gripped my left hand. I looked down at the endless knot inscribed into my skin and saw the golden light run across its length. The smell of lotus flowers filled the room. It was a citrusy green and spicy aroma followed by the sweet smell of wet earth.

"Hello, Simon," she said from behind me. Her melodious voice filled the room and embraced me in warmth and comfort.

I hesitated to turn because she loved startling me with variations of her personifications in an attempt to give me a heart attack.

"I didn't use the mark. Why are you here?" I said, still not looking at her.

"Turn around, we need to talk. This is serious."

"You've said that before and then sprung the death's head on me. We can talk like this, really."

"Simon, turn around."

I sighed and turned, ready for the worst. There was no way I could out-wait her; she was karma and would win eventually. She appeared to be a young woman dressed in casual clothing—blue jeans, comfortable boots and a sweater. Her black hair was short and the smile across her lips reached her hazel eyes. She looked old enough to be a typical college student.

"You look…normal," I said, hesitant that she would morph into some nightmarish entity. "Why are you here?"

"Normal?" she said, looking down at herself. "No such thing. Reality is out of balance."

"Excuse me? That sounds way out of my league. I don't deal in Reality with a capital R. I prefer to stick to lowercase reality."

"The Ferryman is missing. I need you to find him."

The look on my face must have expressed the level of confusion I felt. She never felt explanation was an important part of conversation. I just rolled with the punches and dived in.

"Which Ferryman?"

"*The* Ferryman—Charon," she said.

"The whole River Styx and escorting dead Ferryman?"

"Do you know of another?"

"Why me?"

"Because you are immortal and so unaffected by the upcoming chain of events."

"Well, shit," I said. "Did he just quit?"

"Indeed, copious amounts of it. With Charon not doing his job, souls are being rerouted somehow and it's creating a ripple effect. I don't think he *can* quit. Being the Ferryman is pretty much his raison d'etre."

"Still not seeing how I'm part of this. You need to speak to some of the heavy hitters. Have you tried the gods? Hades, maybe?"

"Don't be dense, Simon," she said as her voice dropped several octaves and she transformed into the Grim Reaper, scythe and all. Her flaming eyes fixed me in place as the bleached white skull drew close to my face and caused my heart to try to exit *through* my chest. "I'm the heaviest hitter of all. I need you to do this. The gods wouldn't know where to start."

She morphed back into the college student and smiled at me. My hands shook slightly, which was exactly the effect she was looking for.

"I hate it when you do that." I sat down on the sofa, careful not to move Chi while she was in a karmic stasis.

"I know," she said and laughed. "You're the only one who reacts that way."

"No. I refuse or decline, or whatever it is, to take this assignment. Find someone else."

"I don't think you understand the gravity of the situation."

"No—you have the wrong person."

It was her turn to look surprised.

"Excuse me?" she said, putting her hands on her hips. "I never get the *wrong person*. In fact in all of history I've never gotten the wrong person."

"Bullshit. You aren't infallible. I've seen plenty of your mistakes. Even fought a few that tried to kill me."

She remained silent for a few heartbeats and I held my breath. Pissing off near omnipotent beings is never a good policy. She took a deep breath, smiled, and remained in college-student form. Thankfully.

"Gods are not immortal, Simon," she whispered as she stepped close. "They thrive on belief. History is rife with the countless deities who have perished or languish in the periphery of the collective consciousness. You, however, are different. You now walk outside of time, independent of belief. This is why I believe you wear my mark."

I subconsciously traced my finger over its subtle contours.

"I don't want your mark, I didn't ask for it."

"Which is why you wear it. I would take it off except I didn't inscribe it into your skin, as you know. Would you like me to try?"

"What does that mean?" I asked warily. "Try what?"

"I can remove the hand, if you like," she said with a smile. "I can't guarantee the mark won't appear elsewhere on your body, though."

"No, thank you. I prefer my limbs attached."

"Let me know if you change your mind. I would be interested in seeing the outcome."

We had already been over this several times. Only the goddess who cursed me could remove the mark. Aside from being one of the most powerful magic-users on the planet, she really knew how to hold a grudge. My habit for getting on the wrong side of the wrong people was fast becoming an art form.

"You need someone with world-ending power, and that's not me. Wait, I know you. What are you leaving out?"

And just like that, I fell into her trap like a rank amateur. She smiled at my words and I knew it was over. She had dangled the bait in front of me and I had bitten down on the hook. Now she would reel me in.

She walked over to where Michiko sat frozen.

"I can see why you feel the way you do," she said, caressing her cheek. "She possesses a deadly beauty, intelligence, and the capacity for breathtaking violence —very similar to the weapon you wield. Does she return your sentiment?"

"Doesn't matter, it could never work between us. She heads the Dark Council and I'm not exactly one of their favorites. Oh, and small detail—she's a vampire?"

"Trivialities," Karma said, waving my words away. "In the face of a love like yours, those are mere excuses —obstacles to be overcome."

"I really hate you right now," I said. "Tell me."

"If you don't find Charon and return him to work, the souls that are left to wander the earth will become enthralled," she said, walking around the room. "They will start another supernatural war to make the last one look like a minor skirmish."

The last supernatural war had almost wiped out humanity. The Dark Council had been formed to prevent another war from ever happening. Its presence created an uneasy truce between the supernatural, human governments, and those who were aware or sensitive enough to realize that there was something more behind the veil.

"The Dark Council would never let that happen," I said, barely believing my own words. "That's the reason they exist—to prevent a war."

"You and I both know there are factions within the Council that would welcome a war to enslave and destroy humanity."

She was right. Some on the Council chafed under the truce with humans. Attacks on the supernatural would be a perfect catalyst.

She looked at Michiko. "They will kill her first, of course," she said.

"Chi can hold her own against the Council. She's probably the most powerful vampire in it," I said, trying to reassure myself.

"They will eliminate her first *because* she is powerful, but power alone is not enough. Even vampires need to sleep. Then they will pursue the imminent threats— magic-users, powerful mages like Tristan."

"Fuck," I whispered.

She had just described the two most important people in my life.

"Once those threats are gone, they will hunt down, destroy, and enslave the humans. It shouldn't take more than a decade or two."

"Can't you do something?"

"I *am* doing something."

"What, me? Are you kidding? This plan of yours is weak at best."

"Have you ever gotten a splinter?" she asked, stepping close.

My mind tripped over the pivot. "Huh? What?"

"A splinter," she said slowly. "Have you ever had

one?"

"Yes, of course, plenty of times."

"When this happened, what did you do? Did you ignore it or divert all attention to removing it?"

She moved over and stood in front of me.

"I removed it. Wait, are you saying I'm the splinter?"

She nodded.

"You're *my* splinter," she said, and poked my chest gently. "And I'm inserting you into this situation."

"Splinters get removed, usually violently."

"I am balance and order. Do you know what people say about me?"

"That you're a bit—?" I started.

"The *other* thing they say about me," she interrupted and narrowed her eyes at me. "My purpose is to reap what you sow. I restore balance and order. I am causality. And you never escape causality."

"Not seeing the connection here. I'm the furthest thing from balance and order I know."

She smiled, and then I knew what she meant.

"Exactly, your very existence refutes my being. You are the chaos to my order. You shouldn't exist and honestly I don't know how it was done, but I know it's tied to me or you wouldn't be wearing my mark."

"Don't you know where he is? Can't you sense Charon?" I asked, looking for an escape route.

"Normally I would, but wherever he's gone I can't feel his presence. You need to go see *him*."

"No way, the last time we spoke, he wanted to kill me, repeatedly—just to see what would happen. He's twisted and sick. I'm immortal, not a masochist."

"He's not so bad once you get to know him."

"I don't *want* to get to know him—at all."

"It's the most logical starting point," she answered, her voice hard. "You have to go see Hades."

"This just went from horrible to nightmarish. How am I supposed to get Hades here? Send him an invite?"

She transformed into a sari-wearing *nanni*, pinched my face, and moved her head in a side-to-side tilt while tutting at me. Her wrists were covered with prayer beads, *malas*, which jangled when she moved.

"I hear he owns property in New York City. If not, you could always visit him at his other—" she began.

"No, not happening, ever," I interrupted. "I'll find him here."

"Take Tristan with you. He's always so pleasant."

"Are we talking about the same Tristan?"

She nodded and smiled at me.

I stared at her, speechless, and she winked at me.

"You will need his help for this."

"What if I can't stop this war? What if I'm not enough?" I whispered.

She straightened out my jacket, jangling the malas as she spoke.

"A word of caution, my splinter. For the short time the mark is active—you're not immortal."

"Which means?"

"There are beings, entities which are not subject to time—like you. When you use the mark, you arouse their curiosity in you. This isn't always a good thing."

"You never answered my question. What if I fail?"

"Oh, the usual—deaths, destruction, the end of life as you know it," she said in a lilting voice. "In the grand scheme of things, this is a pretty big one. Be a good splinter and don't screw up."

She patted my cheek and disappeared.

EIGHT

THE MARK ON my hand began to burn again. I moved back to where I was and faced Michiko as time snapped back and began to flow again.

Chi stared at me as I looked back at her. I could see Yama behind her go slowly Chernobyl as I stood there, mute. It took me a few seconds before I realized Karma did one of her second-to-second stasis moves on me, freezing time in-between two seconds.

"Thank you for preventing my untimely death at the hands of Himayama," I said as I recovered. "What complication?"

"The Council is looking into it, so until I know more she needs to stay with you. Were you able to get blood from the truck?"

I nodded and pulled out a medallion from my pocket. It belonged to one of the hit squad members. I placed it on the table in front of her.

"What clan is this? I don't recognize the crest." Not that I recognized more than two or three of them, but there was no reason to tell her that.

She took the medallion from the table and turned it in her fingers. "You wouldn't. This clan is not very large. After what you did at the garage, they won't strike again anytime soon."

"But they will strike again?"

"Of course. They shunned her and want to see her destroyed. Once they gather enough vampires, they will come for her again."

"Wonderful. Anything else I should know?" I was distracted. My mind was racing about the upcoming meeting with Hades. I needed to plan and tell Monty.

Michiko stood up and took a step toward me. I felt her breath caress my cheek as she spoke. "I apologize for this imposition. It is necessary...for now."

She turned to Yama and said something in Japanese. He bowed to her and responded. She turned back to me, bowed, and disappeared.

I stood there in shock. To my recollection, Michiko had never apologized—to anyone. It meant that whatever 'complication' the Dark Council was dealing with was serious.

"I wonder what that last part was about?" I said, looking at Yama.

He sighed and looked up to the ceiling. I smiled.

"I am to protect you both—with my life," he said in perfect English.

"I feel safer already," I muttered under my breath as he grimaced at me.

Monty walked in and I turned to him. He held up his hand and walked past me. He gave Yama a passing glance and kept moving.

"Tea and sleep. In that order. Whatever it is can wait until morning," he said as he headed into the kitchen.

"Did you deal with them?" I asked.

"That clan is now several members smaller," he said as he tossed about twenty medallions on the kitchen counter. "The blood from the truck will be here in a few hours. I left it with Cecil."

I didn't understand the relationship between Monty and Cecil, the owner of SuNaTran, but I knew it was powerful. If he had the truck, it may as well have never existed.

My phone rang as Monty rummaged in the kitchen. I picked it up on the third ring. You never want to appear too eager.

"Simon, get your ass down to the morgue—now." It was Ramirez. "And bring Tristan."

He hung up.

"Monty—," I started.

"Bloody hell," he replied from the kitchen and slammed a drawer closed. "Let me drink this first and then we can go."

"You need to stay here," I said, looking at Georgianna. "The room to the left is a darkroom. There's a change of clothes in there that should fit you."

"Photography. Is that your hobby?" she asked as she peered into the room.

I shook my head. "Darkroom means no sunlight."

I pressed another number on my phone.

"SuNaTran," said the voice in a crisp English accent. "How can we meet your transportation needs?"

"Hi, Alice," I said, heading to my room. "How

long?"

"Hello, Mr. Strong. Ten minutes?" she replied.

"Perfect," I said and hung up. "Ten minutes, Monty."

A grunt from the kitchen was his reply. I went to my room, removed my ruined suit, and tossed it on my bed. Piero would have a fit if he saw it in its current state. I sighed. There was nothing to be done. It was completely ruined. I shook out the jacket and a wooden mala fell out of one of the jacket pockets with a note attached.

Sometimes a splinter must be a sword, the note read.

I looked it over and counted eighteen beads. They were made of smooth wood and looked worn from constant use. The largest bead held a carved endless knot on two sides. When did she have time to put that in my pocket? Could she pull a stasis within a stasis? I opted not to tumble down that rabbit hole, and put on the mala.

I didn't know what it did and I hoped not to find out anytime soon. If Karma put it in my pocket, she meant for me to wear it, so I did.

Contrary to Piero's fashion advice, I put on a pair of black jeans, my all-purpose hiking boots, and a sweater. I grabbed my leather peacoat because carrying a large blade and a gun is always easier under a coat. I stepped back into the living room just in time to see Georgianna heading to the darkroom.

"There's some food in the fridge," I said mostly to Yama. "If you need anything, you can call either one of us. The darkroom only has that one exit and once the door is closed, nothing short of a tank, or maybe him"—I looked at Yama—"is going to open it. The room itself is a repurposed bank vault."

"Thank you," she said around a yawn. "I know you still have plenty of questions and I promise to answer them when I wake up tonight."

"Fair enough. I'm guessing Yama will stand watch?"

He stared at me and gave a short grunt, master conversationalist that he was. Once she entered, he stood in front of the door and looked about as mobile as Mt. Everest. Between the room and Yama, she was as safe as she could be.

Monty entered the living room and looked at Yama. He stepped up to him and said something in rapid Japanese. Yama opened his eyes wide and bowed as he gave a reply. Monty spoke again before returning the bow. He grabbed his jacket and headed for the door. I followed him out and caught up.

"What did you tell him?" I asked, wondering how many languages he knew. Monty was always full of surprises.

"Nothing of consequence," he said as he put on his suit jacket.

"You didn't offer him dinner, did you? I don't think there's enough food on the eastern seaboard to keep him full."

"When did you get that?" he said, looking at the mala on my wrist.

"Not too long ago," I said as I held it up. "I'll explain on the way. What did you say?"

"I told him I was an eighth dan in Go and would be willing to enjoy a game with him," he said as we entered the lobby. "He was honored I would extend the invitation."

"And? What else?"

Because I knew him well enough to know he wouldn't let it rest there.

"I told him I knew he served your vampire. If he failed in his duty to protect a shunned vampire, a task he may consider dishonorable and beneath him, I'd personally take care of him before she did. I promised him a coward's death."

It was in these moments that I was relieved Monty was my friend.

"You got all of that in those few sentences?"

"In Japanese, what's unspoken is louder than what's said. Now tell me, when did *she* appear and how much shite are we in?"

NINE

SUPERNATURAL TRANSPORTATION, OR SuNaTran for short, provided a car service for the supernatural population. Because being covered in blood and viscera and hailing a cab, even one in New York City—the capital of the bizarre—will get you cuffed and sitting in a NYTF cell.

SuNaTran provided discreet service any time of day or night to any of the five boroughs and beyond—for a price. The transportation they provided—and I use the term loosely since each Rolls Royce Phantom was a tank disguised as a car—was the height in security.

By the time we stood outside the Moscow, Robert had pulled up silently in the black Phantom. Each of SuNaTran's drivers was highly trained. They could execute tight J-turns and other evasion-style techniques to ensure the safety of their passengers.

The bottomless pit known as the trunk was dubbed Pandora's Box because it contained just a little of everything and was all designed to cause pain or explode, and in most cases, both.

With a push of a button, Robert opened the doors as we approached. He was the only driver I knew in the years we had used SuNaTran. He was stockily built, with quick eyes and lightning-fast reflexes.

"Robert," I said, and nodded when we got inside. "Morgue please."

"Yes, sir, Mr. Strong. Right away," he said with a slight accent.

"Cut the formality. It's us, Simon and Tristan."

"Yes, sir, Mr. Strong," he said, tipping his cap and completely ignoring my direct request.

"One day I'll get him to slip up," I said to Monty, who had found the cookies—or biscuits, as he called them—and was looking through the selection of teas.

"Won't happen," Monty replied and chose some tea from the kettle placed strategically on the sideboard. "He drove for a member of British aristocracy, a Duke or Earl of some kind. They practically invented formality. You can't teach an old dog new tricks."

I sank back in the luxurious seat and closed my eyes for a few seconds. It didn't last long before I heard the short cough. I opened my eyes to Monty sipping his tea and looking at me, waiting.

"She came by this afternoon before you got back," I said as I sat up and readjusted. "She did one of those karmic stasis things where she stops time and then has a heart-to-heart, usually stopping mine."

"Did you use the mark?" he asked in between sips.

"No, I had just gotten back and Chi was inside the living room with Yama the Mountain. There was no imminent threat."

"Except for the Dark Council vampire and her giant in the living room."

"Exactly. Well, I guess Yama could have stomped on me, but it wasn't imminent."

He placed the teacup down and nibbled on a biscuit.

"Did you know that Yama means mountain in Japanese?" he said, picking up a second biscuit. "It also means restraint and self-control. Try to use some the next time you're around him. Don't antagonize him more than necessary. What did she want?"

I shared everything Karma had told me and explained how I found the mala in my jacket pocket after she had gone.

"May I see it?" he asked, extending his hand.

I took it off and gave it to him. He held and examined it. He touched each of the smooth wooden beads and focused on the largest one. He rubbed the endless knot and the mala glowed white as it shot forward and buried his body into the seat, knocking the air out of him. The car fishtailed as Robert fought to keep it under control. Several tires screeched behind us as he pulled to the side and lowered the partition.

"Everything all right, sirs?" he said, nonplussed.

Monty was still catching his breath. He waved his hand and nodded.

"It's all good, Bobby," I said, waving my hand in front of my face. "I think Monty had some bad tea, you know?"

Robert raised the partition without a word in response. The car pulled out a few seconds later.

"Bloody hell," Monty said as he gasped, rubbing his chest and holding out the mala to me. "It seems to be some kind of shield or repulsor."

"It didn't like you," I said as I took it and placed it back on my wrist. I held it out away from me for few seconds just in case it decided to launch itself again.

"It wasn't made for *me*. That much is clear."

"I can see where this can come in handy. Especially on the subway in the morning," I said, holding up my wrist and looking at the mala.

"Did she say she couldn't sense Charon, or that he felt hidden?"

"She said she couldn't feel his presence and then pointed me to Hades."

"Really," he said, rubbing his chin.

"Remember him? Big, powerful, scary god? Likes dead things?"

"She's right. It makes the most sense to see him first. I wonder if any of the other psychopomps have gone missing."

"The psycho—what?"

The car came to a stop and the doors opened before Monty could answer. Robert lowered the partition.

"Will you need me to wait, sirs?"

"No, thank you, Robert. Please pass on my thanks to Cecil when you return," Monty said as we stepped out of the Phantom.

Robert tipped his cap and raised the partition. He drove away as we entered 520 1st Avenue, which was also the OCME, or Office of the Chief Medical Examiner. I just knew it as the morgue. I noticed the unmarked NYTF car across the street as we approached the building.

"Ramirez must be sitting on something serious if

he's dragging us down here before noon," I said, looking at my watch.

"I thought three squad cars was suspect," Monty said as we headed past the outer vestibule.

"Three? I only saw one."

"Two more around the corner," he said, pointing. "Trying and failing to be subtle."

I looked through the glass and saw the unmarked squad NYTF cruisers sitting halfway down the block.

Monty opened the door and we entered the oblong-shaped building. I pressed the call button for the elevator and looked around. The NYTF officer standing in the lobby was doing his best to blend in, but I found his location a little strange.

We entered the elevator and headed down to the third sub-basement reserved for supernatural deaths. When the doors opened, two more NYTF officers standing guard by the elevator greeted us. We flashed our credentials, courtesy of Ramirez, and walked down to the autopsy room.

The smell of chemicals permeated the space and I had to hold my breath for a few seconds as I adjusted. Fluorescent lights kept the room brightly illuminated. Three stainless steel tables dominated the center of the room. Scales hung at the head of each, reminding me of the old hanging meat scales used in butcher shops. Next to each of the autopsy tables sat trays with silver instruments. On the far wall, a sink ran the length of the room.

A body lay on the center table. It was strapped down and held in place with runic restraints, which were similar to the silver cuffs we used on the werewolf, only stronger. Ramirez stood against the far wall with his arms crossed and a scowl on his face. Two more NYTF officers were on the other side of the room with their hands resting on their holsters. They looked twitchy, which made me nervous.

Allen, the Medical Examiner, stood over the body on the table. He wore light blue scrubs and a white T-shirt. His gray hair was loose and peeked out from under his cap. His glasses were thick enough to make his eyes look larger than they were, reminding me of Marty Feldman. He was somewhere between a mad scientist and Dr. Frankenstein, but he was the best coroner in the city, and a friend.

"Simon, Tristan, your timing is perfect," Allen said, moving quickly around the table. "Please stand over there next to Officer Ramirez, and don't move."

"What was so urgent you needed us here at this hour? This couldn't wait until tonight?" I asked, irritated. The morgue and cemeteries were high on my 'things to avoid' list.

"Watch," Ramirez said, gesturing to the table and looking a little green.

I looked at Monty and saw him flex his jaw. His hands were formed into fists and I could feel the tension coming off him.

"What is it? What's wrong?" I asked, but he ignored me. I followed where he was looking and saw him staring at the body.

"That rune," he said to Allen, his voice steel, "where did you get it?"

"Easy, Tristan," Ramirez said. "He got it from us."

The two officers in the back shifted their focus

slightly to include Monty, and I didn't like it. They were acting spooked and that usually resulted in someone shooting first and asking questions second. I stepped into what would be their line of fire if they aimed at Monty and looked closely at the disc Allen was handling. It was about the size of a small plate, and golden. Inscribed on both sides, I could make out a few symbols but couldn't decipher its meaning.

Allen had it resting on the corpse's chest. Next to the body sat a small container covered in runes. The outside of the container held more runes I didn't understand.

"I've never seen those symbols. What does it do?" I whispered to Monty.

"It's a rune of negation. They were created to combat mages, sorcerers, and wizards."

"How does it do that?"

"Proximity to that rune will suppress any magic in the area around it," he said, stepping closer to the table. "It creates a magic dead zone. If the rune is activated, it will negate everything in a five-hundred-foot radius."

"What do you mean activated? Wait—negate everything?"

He nodded. "Including us," he said and flexed his fingers.

"Does that mean that your magic is—?" I started.

"It was created by the Golden Circle. All the negation runes were, during the last war."

"Isn't that your—?"

He cut me off with a look. "Which is why I still possess my powers around it."

I could see a light covering of sweat forming on his

brow.

"Is that all it does? Shut off magic?"

"And undo everything around it if active—yes, that's all," he said and gave me another look.

"So this one isn't active?" I asked, looking at it warily.

"If it were, we would be standing in a dead space devoid of anything," he said. "Right now it's exhibiting its dormant nature."

"This is the equivalent of a magical nuke," I said, taking a step back from the table. "It seems like overkill."

"Under the right circumstances, placing that rune on a person with an affinity to magic would kill them instantly. Those things are supposed to be kept in their containers in a sealed vault," Monty said, looking at Ramirez.

"Why not destroy it? It sounds more dangerous than helpful," I said.

"Because of situations like this," Ramirez whispered. "Now, watch."

Allen stepped on a pedal and began speaking into a microphone suspended from a chain attached to the ceiling.

"Subject is Brian Matthews, male, Caucasian, approximately twenty-five years old. No visible contusions or lacerations. Cause of death appears to be GSW to the neck causing hemorrhage from right carotid artery."

"Who shot him?" I asked Ramirez.

He looked over at the officers on the other side of the room and pointed with his chin.

"They were on patrol last night when this guy

incinerates some vic on the spot," he said. "Said his eyes were all over the place and it looked like he was on something. Then he killed one officer and critically injured another."

"He's a mage? I thought mages didn't go around barbecuing people. Isn't he kind of young to have that much power?"

"He's a sorcerer," Monty answered and shifted his weight while he unbuttoned his jacket. "They tap into a different, darker, source of power. Mages don't go around incinerating people—without provocation. Probably an enforcer. Low level, from the look of it."

"He looks Dark Council to me," I said. "But why use a sorcerer? They usually use vampires on the hit squad."

"'Resolution Teams,'" Monty corrected.

"Sure, whatever," I said. "Never heard of them using magic-users to 'resolve' a situation—unless the target was—?"

"A magic-user," Monty finished as he flexed his fingers.

"Please pay attention," Allen said to us and then turned back to the microphone. "Removing negation rune procured from the NYTF from subject's chest."

Allen picked up the rune from sorcerer's chest and placed it in the container. The body on the table convulsed and his eyes shot open.

The two officers drew their guns and cursed.

"Stand down!" yelled Ramirez. "Both of you, outside—now."

They complied and left the room as they holstered their weapons. Monty's hands were covered in black energy but he remained where he stood, looking at what used to be a corpse. I pulled my coat to one side to give me access to the Ebonsoul. Ramirez had pulled his gun and held it at his side.

"Allen, explain what's going on here," I said, because now I felt as twitchy as the officers looked. "He was dead a second ago and now he's not."

"Actually he was in a type of stasis," Allen answered while adjusting his glasses. "The negation rune only stopped him while it was in contact with his body. Once removed, well, you can see for yourself—he doesn't appear to stay dead. Just like someone I know."

"Not funny, Allen," I said and jumped back when Brian tried to get up.

"Where the hell am I?" Brian asked from the table. "Who are you?"

He tugged on the runic restraints. They gave off a dull orange glow but kept him strapped down.

"You're in the morgue," I said and eyed the restraints. "What do you remember?"

"The morgue?" He was clearly confused and he shook his head. "I had to fulfill an obligation for the Council and I caught up to my target near Central Park. I thought I managed to surprise him before he could hit me with anything, but he was too fast."

"What did he do?" I asked.

"He cast a spell, something that hit me like a bucket of ice," he replied, and shuddering. "So I fried him where he stood. That's all I remember, until now."

"Let me fill in the gaps for you," Ramirez said, pulling out a pad. "You were approached by four NYTF officers, two who were patrolling the park at the time."

"I don't remember any officers around," Brian said. "It was just me and the target."

"Doesn't ring a bell?" Ramirez said. "They asked you to stand down and you replied with a" —he looked at his notes—"'black glob of goo' that killed one of the officers."

"Where did *you* learn an entropy spell?" Monty said, each word a veiled threat. "That's way beyond your skill level."

"That's a lie," Brian said, and tugged against the restraints again. "Why would I attack NYTF?"

"Murdering a target with magic comes to mind," Ramirez answered. "At best you were looking at a cell. At worst, erasure of all abilities and death. Might make someone do something desperate."

"I didn't attack any officers!" Brian yelled. "I don't even know what an entropy spell is."

Ramirez nodded and reached for the laptop that was on the table to the right.

"In light of your present undead state, I thought you might say that, so we managed to download the bodycam footage," he said. "Tell me if anyone looks familiar."

Ramirez pressed a few buttons on the laptop and the screen came to life. An image of one of the lower entrances of the park came into view. Brian stood in the middle of two officers. The camera jerked rapidly for about two seconds, then a moment later one of the officers began screaming as he was covered in what looked like black pudding. The other officer jumped back and fired several times.

One of the bullets hit Brian in the neck and he hit the ground. Another officer silvered him as he bled out. Placing the restraints on Brian probably saved their lives since not more than ten seconds later Brian was up again and attacked the closest officer. Without magic, he was only able to use his fists. They subdued him and put him in the back of one of the cruisers.

"Recognize anyone?" Ramirez asked as he pointed to the computer screen. "See anyone you know?"

Brian shook his head and then his eyes went white. He pulled on the restraints, ripping them apart. His hands were covered in a black gelatinous substance. Allen fumbled to get the rune out of its container. He managed to pull it partway out as Brian flung some of the black goop at him. The gelatin landed on his arm and burned its way down to the bone as he screamed and fell back. He dropped the container and it slid under the table.

"Fools!" Brian said, only it wasn't Brian's voice but something deeper, making the hairs on the back of my neck stand on end. "You can't stop me. My time is coming. Your end is near."

The officers from outside were rushing in with guns drawn as I pulled the Ebonsoul out of its sheath. We were all too slow—except Monty. He hit Brian with two orbs of darkness that dissolved him into nothingness. The orbs even ate away part of the table he sat on.

"What the fuck!" one of the officers said. "What the hell was that thing?"

I checked his badge; it said "Thomas." He seemed to be the most skittish of the group so I let Monty deal with him. I stepped over to Ramirez, who was holstering his weapon. His jaw flexed as he looked at what remained of the table. One of the forensic assistants came in and tended to Allen, cleaning the wound and bandaging his arm.

"Tell me you can explain this, Simon, because in all my years in the NYTF I've never seen anything like this," he said, and wiped his face. "And I have seen some bizarre piss-in-your-pants shit."

His hands shook to match the trembling in his voice.

"Ramirez, I don't know what I just saw, but we both know there's more out there than we can explain. Let me look into it and see what I can find out."

"You'd better move on this quick," he said as he grabbed my arm. "I've got brass telling me to open the vaults—just in case."

"That's not good. Those vaults need to stay closed."

"Not if dead sorcerers are running around the city," he said. "I don't need to tell you what happens if this gets out to the public."

"That sorcerer was enthralled," Monty said calmly as he came over after speaking with the officer. "It takes considerable power to enthrall a corpse, much less one possessed of magic."

"What the hell did you hit him with?" Ramirez whispered. "Those things ate right through him."

"A disintegration spell," Monty replied and buttoned his jacket. "You have to keep these occurrences away from the public."

"People are smart, but mobs are stupid. It'll start a panic," I said as I rested my hand on the Ebonsoul.

"A panic that will lead to war," Ramirez said, his

voice grim. "We won't survive a second supernatural war. We can't let that happen."

He bent down and grabbed the container with the rune inside. He made sure it was secure, and he left the room.

"This is just the beginning," Monty said, looking at the destroyed table that had held the sorcerer. "It's going to get worse."

It was time to see Hades.

TEN

THE OFFICES OF Terra Sur Global Mining occupied the top ten floors of One New York Plaza, an office building located downtown on Water Street. We grabbed a cab and looped around the bottom of the island. Monty stopped me when we got out of the cab.

"Are you certain he's here?" he asked, looking up at the building. "Let me do the speaking. It's not like you two are cordial."

"I did some digging around. Terra Sur Global is owned by several shell companies, but they all point back to the Pluto Conglomerate, which is owned by him and has their main office—here."

I followed Monty's gaze up the building, and a feeling of dread grabbed my stomach and started river dancing. He gave me a sidelong glance.

"It's a bit obvious, isn't it?" he said, looking around. "I mean why would he have an office here of all places?"

"I had to call in a few favors from The Hack, just to

get this much. This place doesn't even officially exist."

"You mean that insufferable little snot?" Monty said with a look of disgust. "I don't know why you entertain that child and his rants. What kind of name is 'The Hack'?"

"That *child* happens to be one of the most dangerous cybercriminals I've ever encountered. Every three-letter agency on the planet fears and admires him."

"Are you certain you want to do this?" he asked, a look of genuine concern on his face. "Hades isn't someone to trifle with and his power puts him in an entirely different league from what we're used to dealing with."

"No, I don't *want* to do this, but I *have* to," I said. "Besides, we need to find Charon and Hades is our best chance."

We entered the lobby and were stopped by security next to the massive wooden reception desk, designed to make you feel puny. We placed our credentials on the desk and told the receptionist we needed access to the tenth floor. She looked at us over her glasses from behind the redwood posing as a desk as she made a call. With her sky-blue eyes and almost white blond hair, she could have easily been Olga's sister and probably came from the same region.

"Russian?" I said, using my most debonair voice.

Monty groaned beside me and pinched the bridge of his nose.

She gave me a withering look, punched some keys, and looked down at a monitor embedded beneath the surface of the desk. Apparently she was immune to my wiles.

"No one is allowed upstairs without an appointment," she said, looking at Monty. "Do you have one?"

"No, but I'm sure he'll make an exception," I said, leaning into her field of vision. "I'm a huge fan."

Monty nudged me gently in the side with an elbow and almost cracked a rib.

"Tristan Montague, Esquire," Monty said, introducing himself with an extended hand that she shook. "Please inform your employer that it's of the utmost importance that we speak with him."

"One moment," she said with a brief smile as we stepped several paces away from the desk. She pressed some more keys and picked up the phone next to her.

"Esquire? Since when? Are you some kind of English noble?" I whispered.

"Since now, and shut it," he whispered back. "Do you want to speak to him or not?"

"Yes, we need to. He's our best and only lead right now."

"Then let me do this, or I swear I'll hold you down and let the angry Valkyrie behind the desk swat you," he said while staring straight ahead.

"Monty, you kinky dog you," I said. "Now that you mention it, she does look a bit Nordic."

"Mr. Montague?" she said with another smile as we approached the desk. "Your escort will arrive shortly. Please have a seat. Would you care for some refreshments while you wait?"

She handed back our wallets and pointed to the large waiting area comprised of dark leather sofas, an oversized Persian rug, and several idle laptop stations.

"Yes, thank you. Tea—Earl Grey, no sugar," he said and headed off to the waiting area.

"I would love a coffee, grande white mocha, please, hold the whipped cream," I said. "Can you make sure they stir the mocha? If not it just gunks up on the bottom and then it just tastes like sludge."

"Of…course," she said and picked up the phone. "Two teas, Earl Grey, no sugar, and hold the whipped cream."

She stared daggers at me and it was clear I had won her over. Another victim to the Strong charm. I sighed and then walked over to the waiting area and sat across from Monty.

"It's clear they need to work on their people skills," I said, "but I can tell she's crushing hard on me."

"Is there a lack of oxygen in this reality called Simon's universe? The real question is: Why would Hades have a Valkyrie in his employ?"

"Wait, you're serious? She's a *real* Valkyrie?"

He nodded absentmindedly. "This could be a result of Charon's disappearance," he said and remained silent as the tea arrived. The server could've been a twin to the woman behind the desk. I noticed my cup was mysteriously absent. He continued speaking once she left. "They are known as the choosers of the slain and if Hades is shorthanded, they could be acting as surrogate psychopomps. It still doesn't explain how that sorcerer became enthralled, though."

He drank his tea, closed his eyes, and took a deep breath.

"This fixation you have with tea is like some weird porn. Why don't you move over to a real drink and try coffee? Put some hair on your chest. You could even sound sophisticated and call it café noir."

He stared at me for a few seconds before taking another sip.

"Because my palate is accustomed to eating my beans, not roasting, grinding, and then drinking them," he said and put his cup down. "When you're ready to join civilization, I'll introduce you to tea."

I was about to ask him once again what a psychopomp was when another tall blonde glided over to where we sat. When I saw her, it started to give Monty's Valkyrie theory some weight. She stood several inches over my six feet and looked like she could bench press me without breaking a sweat. She wore a dark blue business suit with matching heels. From my experience with Piero, I could tell it wasn't off-the-rack. It almost looked like fine chainmail. She gave me a cursory glance and focused on Monty.

"If you would follow me, please," she said and headed back the way she came.

I walked next to her and noticed her gait. If she was a personal assistant, I was a ballerina. I could see the extensive training in every step and shift of bodyweight. No motion was wasted as we walked. This woman was a warrior.

We stepped into the elevator and I touched her arm lightly. She looked down at my hand and shifted her eyes to my face with a smile that said she would be happy to remove my arm if I had grown tired of having two.

"Can I ask?" I said, and sensed Monty get in rib-striking range. "What are you?"

"Of course you can ask," she said and kept that smile on her face.

I saw Monty roll his eyes and shake his head.

"You must excuse him," he said, giving me a stare. "He has an acute case of stupidity."

She nodded and turned to face me. Her eyes went from cool blue to black with red pupils.

"I choose the slain on the battlefield," she said softly and moved a few inches closer. "Maybe one day I will choose you."

The temperature in the elevator dropped by about twenty degrees and I could see my breath on every exhalation. I took a step back to admire the effect. I mistakenly thought my encounters with Karma had prepared me for these transformations; I was wrong. I kept a calm façade while my heart was trying to climb out of my ribcage.

"No, thanks," I said with a slight tremble in my voice. "I'm spoken for and she doesn't like to share."

This time Monty really did slam me in the ribs and I had to cough to catch my breath. The elevator reached the top floor and the doors slid apart, revealing a long hallway. Set on the wall opposite the elevator was the Terra Sur logo. A T intersected an S in a gothic font, with the bottom of the T ending in a drill bit. In the center, where the letters met, was a diamond half the size of my fist.

She exited and led the way down the hallway to a set of large double doors.

"Do *not* antagonize Hades," Monty whispered as we followed. "We need his help."

She stopped at the doors, opened one for us, and

held it as we approached the cavernous office.

"Your friend gives you good advice. Heed it," she said with a short nod. "Your words will cause you immeasurable grief one day."

I gave her a short bow. "It's a gift," I said as I followed Monty into the hangar-sized office. At the far end was another redwood-sized desk. On both walls to either side of the desk were large screens broken up into several dozen displays.

The desk itself held two clusters of monitors made up of six screens each. The fourth wall, behind the desk, was made up of one massive window-wall. The afternoon sunlight bathed the room in a warm haze. Another Terra Sur logo adorned the right wall, complete with an unbelievable diamond.

"Are those things real?" I said as I pointed to the apple-sized stone in the middle of the logo. This one was larger than the one in the hallway, and it refracted the sunlight that washed over the logo.

Monty ignored me as we trekked across another large Persian rug. This one dwarfed the one in the lobby and covered the floor of the office from wall to wall. My feet sank into it as we walked. By the time we were close to the desk, my calves burned from the exertion. It was like walking on sand.

Behind the massive desk sat Hades. There was no smoke or lightning surrounding him, much to my disappointment. He wore a black bespoke suit that probably cost more than all my suits combined. His gray shirt had a hint of rose in it and was complemented by the pastel rose-colored tie.

He sported a goatee where I expected a Fu Manchu

beard. His moderately long hair rested against his shoulders. He looked like any other successful CEO of a large multinational corporation.

Behind Hades stood Corbel Nwobon, his head of Cerberus Security. The file The Hack had given me on him was thin. He was a ghost. He was an averaged-sized man with an above-average intellect, if the rumors were true. Wherever Hades was, Corbel was always nearby.

I didn't think Hades needed any kind of security, though. No one was insane enough to try to attack him directly. Corbel's reputation as the 'Hound of Hades' was fearsome enough to be an additional deterrent, though.

I could see him ticking off a mental checklist about our threat level when I opened my coat. He dismissed me after a few seconds and gave Monty a longer glance before looking away. We must have rated high on the 'insignificant motes of dust' scale.

"Tristan, Simon, please have a seat," Hades said, placing a steaming cup of coffee on the desk. His voice, a deep bass, resonated throughout the office. For a second, I thought James Earl Jones had entered behind us, and I almost turned around.

He sat with his fingers steepled and elbows resting lightly on the arms of his chair. In front of his desk sat three large wingback chairs upholstered in rich, dark brown leather. Monty and I avoided the center chair.

"Are these Harrisons?" Monty asked, running his hands over the leather. "They must be."

It was my turn to roll my eyes. Monty always lost it around anything remotely English.

Hades nodded and smiled. "You know your chairs," he said, taking a sip from his cup full of caffeinated ambrosia. "I had them imported from the UK direct. But I assume you didn't come here to discuss interior design. So, how can I help you?"

"Actually we're here to help you," Monty said while removing some lint from his sleeve. "We understand you are having an issue regarding the Ferryman?"

"What are you referring to?"

My bullshitometer was pinging all over the place. Red flags were flying left and right. Any time a god answered your question with a question and feigned ignorance, it usually signaled imminent death.

I opened my jacket just in case I needed to access the Ebonsoul. I didn't know if it would have any effect on him, but if I was going down it was going to be swinging.

"How many Ferrymen do you know escort dead souls?" I asked.

"Simon," he said, grabbing my attention, "how *is* Kali doing these days? Is she still upset with you?"

The mark on my hand itched at the mention of her name.

"She has a long memory," I said, rubbing my hand against the chair. "I haven't seen her in five years. We don't really talk much."

"That's a shame," Hades said as he shook his head. "You should really keep in touch with those who hold a special place in your life."

"Since when did Odin lend you the Valkyries?" Monty asked.

"Pardon?" Hades said with a slight edge. He made a

gesture with his hand and Corbel headed for the door.
He gave me a look as he crossed the floor and I
returned it with my best Clint Eastwood stare. He
seemed unfazed, looked at Hades, and gave him a short
nod as he opened the door and stepped out of the
office.

I turned back to Hades.

"You heard him," I said as I leaned back. "The
Valkyries. Why are they here?"

"Because I requested them," he said, and the voice in
the back of my head that was warning me earlier began
yelling now about getting out now while I still could.

The only thing worse than evasion from a god was
their blunt honesty.

"I didn't realize you guys cross-pantheoned," I said.
"I mean, Odin and the Valkyries are Norse, and you're
Greek. I thought there were strict rules about all of
you, you know, speaking?"

"The depth of your ignorance is nearly fathomless,"
Hades said, and took another sip. His eyes followed
mine. "Would you like some? It's an excellent blend
from the South—guaranteed to give you that much
needed jolt."

That little voice broke out the megaphone and began
screaming—NO. Then I remembered something about
accepting food from Hades being a bad idea.

"No, thanks. I'll pass," I said reluctantly.

"To answer your pantheon question, we don't
conform to any rules imposed on us by humans,
supernatural or otherwise."

"We just came from the morgue," Monty said,
unwavering. "And a credible source told us that Charon

is missing."

"Your credible source was at the morgue?" Hades asked with a smile. "I thought only I spoke with the dead."

"Karma," I said, and let the word just hang there.

"I'm familiar with the concept, yes," he said and pulled off a genuine stare that put mine to shame. "Are you threatening me?"

In that second, wrapped up in the briefest of moments, I saw the chink in his armor as his façade slipped about a hair's breadth. Monty noticed the opening, shifted in his expensive English chair, and pounced.

"Who would be insane enough to threaten you?" Monty asked. "I mean besides Simon."

I smiled at Hades, but I felt the power emanating from him. It took every ounce of will I possessed not to run out of the office in fear. The voice clawing in the back of my brain had stopped yelling and was now curled up and sobbing about how I was going to die for pissing off a god.

"Your blade is useless against me," Hades said, fixing me with his gaze. "You are an ant attempting to attack an elephant."

"A swarm of ants can bring down just about anything," I replied, returning his stare. "Even an elephant."

"True," he said, pushing back from his desk and standing. He turned his back on us and looked out the window-wall. "But you aren't a swarm of anything, except perhaps annoyance. I only see the two of you."

He had a point.

"Karma, with a capital K, told me Charon is missing," I said, undeterred. "Are you in the habit of giving your employees vacations?"

"Karma. The one we can't escape," he said, tugging on his goatee. "Why would she bother with you? Ah, your mark—Kali *was* clever."

"What do you mean?" I asked, and sat up suddenly curious. "What did Kali do?"

"You'll have to ask her. Maybe you should look her up? I can give you her last known location, if you like."

"No, thanks," I said. "Trying to focus on *your* missing Ferryman."

"Charon was recently tasked with a very unique role," Hades said after a pause. "As the oldest, he was the only one strong enough to gather a special group of souls."

"He was collecting the souls of sorcerers," Monty whispered. "Powerful ones."

Hades nodded. "Your reputation as detectives is well earned," he said and turned to face us.

"Why would you have Charon collect the souls of sorcerers? What makes them special?" I asked.

"Not only sorcerers. Those magic-users with a special affinity for magic at a certain caliber."

"Why would he abandon his post, though?" Monty asked. "Is it possible one of these souls overpowered him?"

"He, like you, Simon, is immune to magic-based attacks," Hades answered, revealing he knew more about me than I thought. "And he would *never* abandon his post."

"But he's missing. And we just came from the

morgue where one of your highly calibrated souls tried to end us—*after* he was dead," I said leaning forward.

"Are you certain he was dead?" Hades asked. "Death, like life, can be a tricky thing."

"He wore a rune of negation created by the Golden Circle and managed to reanimate upon its removal, even after it was on his body for a prolonged period," Monty replied. "If he wasn't dead before its placement, he should've been once it rested on him."

"A Golden Circle rune, you say?" Hades replied as he drummed his fingers on the desk. "Isn't that your sect, Tristan? Was he in possession of his faculties?"

"*Was* my sect. Initially, yes, he was lucid," Monty said. "Right up until the attack. Then he appeared enthralled."

"Appeared?" I said. "He was a puppet. Someone or something was pulling the strings, and it was pissed."

"This changes things," Hades said and gestured again.

Behind us, the door opened and I saw Corbel standing just inside the entrance.

"Yes, sir?" he said. "How may I serve?"

"The situation has escalated. Take them to Thanatos."

"Wait, isn't Thanatos… death?"

"That would be Death with a capital D," he said. "I'm sensing apprehension from you, Simon. Why should that concern you?"

"I just heard he wasn't all that friendly," I answered. "As in, he hates humans."

"He isn't, but don't worry, he hates gods with the same intensity he hates humans."

"So you don't know where Charon is?" I asked. "Why not just say so and save us time?"

"Bloody hell, Simon," Monty whispered under his breath. "Let's refrain from angering the god, shall we?"

"My offer still stands, Simon," Hades said and flashed me a predatory smile while he sat back down. "I would enjoy nothing more than to spend a day or two with you—testing the limits of your *gift*. Consider my invitation a standing one. Corbel, you may take them."

He turned his chair to face the window and we were effectively dismissed.

"Yes, sir," Corbel said. "With me, please."

"Thank you for your time," Monty said and headed for the door.

"Tristan," Hades said as we crossed the ocean of carpet, "you asked if anyone would be insane enough to threaten me or my position."

"Yes, I did," Monty answered, pausing for a moment to look at him. "But I figured it's a rhetorical question. You're the Zeus of the underworld."

"It's not rhetorical," Hades answered with a tight smile. "Speak to Thanatos."

ELEVEN

CORBEL LED US out of the office. Monty was deep
in thought as we headed to the elevator.

"Why is he sending us to Thanatos?" I asked.
"Doesn't he rule the underworld?"

"Charon reports directly to Thanatos," Corbel
replied as he walked past the elevator bank to a door at
the far end of the hall. "Thanatos reports to Hades as a
personification of death."

The door we came to was made of a dark wood. On
it rested a diamond-shaped brass plaque. In the center
of the plaque, in bas-relief, was a large letter A with a
winged man beneath it. On the upper sides of the
diamond, I could read Arkangel Industries.

Corbel pointed to the door. "This is as far as I go,"
he said and took a step back. "A word of advice:
Thanatos doesn't like visitors, even those announced by
Hades. He especially dislikes long-lived ones. Feels
you're gaming the system. If you want to walk out of
there again, let the mage do the talking."

He turned around and walked back to Hades's office.

"Well, that was cheery," I said, looking for a doorknob. "You ready?"

Monty was still lost in thought. "Before we go in and speak with him, we may need to reframe our thinking."

"What do you mean?"

"What if Charon is not missing?"

"So, what, he quit and forgot to tell his boss?" I asked. "It's not like he can just take a few days off, go on a long weekend to—where would a soul transporter go?"

"No," Monty said. "If he's not missing—"

"Then someone grabbed him," I finished. "Who could do that?"

"I think the better question is who would profit from it?"

Monty placed his hand on the plaque and the door unlocked, opening inward with a creak.

I could have sworn my brain seized as we looked inside. I stopped and looked back to the hallway, with the gleaming wood and metal finishes. The huge diamond from the Terra Sur logo gleamed and glinted in the light. I looked back in and saw the inside of a New York delicatessen.

The first thing I noticed was the smell of pastrami wafting through the air and grabbing my nostrils as we walked in.

"What the hell is going on?" I asked Monty, pulling him close. "Why are we standing in a deli?"

"It appears Thanatos is also Azrael," Monty said, as if the sentence made sense. "Or in this case Ezrael."

I looked around and knew where we were, but still

couldn't believe it.

"This is clear across town and doesn't look like it should be called 'Arkangel' anything." I looked around and took in the scene. "Death hangs out in Katz's Deli?"

Photos of celebrities covered the walls. Small tables, which sat four, filled most of the floor space. Some of the tables were occupied with patrons either eating or having lively conversations. A large wooden counter ran across one wall with men behind it who were serving drinks or food.

A bearded man dressed in a white shirt with black pants and a black vest was sitting in a corner alone. He was poring over a thick book. Monty made a beeline for his table and pulled out a chair.

"May we join you?" he said, looking at the older man.

The old man didn't bother to look up and motioned for us to sit down. I grabbed the other chair and sat across from what appeared to me to be an old Jewish scholar. Monty peered across the table at the book and raised an eyebrow.

"Why would *you* need to read the *Zohar*?" he asked.

"Don't you mean why are we sitting in a deli?" I said, confused. "Who is this and where is Arkangel Industries?"

"Stop being such a kvetch," the old man said and looked at me. "Such a pain in the tochus."

The yarmulke he wore was covered in runes that gave off a faint glow as he read his book. I almost reached out and touched it, but Monty gave me a stink-eye and I decided against it.

"This is Ezrael, also known as Azrael or the Angel of death," Monty said, "or Death for short—with a capital D."

The old man waved the words away. "So many names, Ezra is fine," he said and closed the tome. "The deli is because there is no greater expression of life than sitting in one and having pastrami on rye. Besides, Willy said I could borrow the décor. I tried to keep it as authentic as possible."

"Is this the real deli?" I asked. "Or some dimensional replica?"

"Oh, it's real and it isn't," Ezra answered without answering. "You go out that door" —he pointed at the exit—"and you'll find yourself on 2nd Avenue."

"Ezra, Hades sent us to you," Monty started. "About Charon."

"I know," Ezra said, and closed the book. "Have you eaten?"

He pulled a waiter walking by our table.

"I could eat," I said as the smells wrapped themselves around my head and created a chain reaction in my stomach that resulted in a loud rumble. "Sorry."

"Two pastrami on rye with mustard. And bring them some sour pickles and an egg cream for this one," he said, pointing at me. "You can thank me later."

The waiter took off and left us alone.

"Pastrami? Ezra, I really don't—" Monty began.

"Eat meat, I know. This won't violate your diet or your energy management."

"We really shouldn't," Monty said. "We can't stay long. We have to—"

Ezra just stared at Monty until he ran out of words. An event that had never happened in my lifetime.

"It seems neither of you will be having a final meeting with me for a long time," Ezra said. "You" — he pointed at Monty—"because of magic. And you" —he looked in my direction with a squint—"because you wanted to be a shamus with that meshuggah, Kali, and she cursed you."

"I had no idea she would react that way, really," I said. "In my defense, Shiva said I…Forget it."

"Here's what we're going to do," Ezra said, moving his book to an adjacent table. "And by 'we' I mean you. You two are going to enjoy your lunch—on the house. Then you're going to be a pair of mensches and find Charon before we are completely schtupped."

"Do you have any idea why he would leave his post?" Monty asked. "Or was it something else?"

Ezra rubbed his index finger across his nose and pointed at Monty. The waiter arrived at our table with enough food to feed five people, or one Yama, I imagined.

"I don't usually accept visitors, but you two, I like," Ezra said and pushed back his chair. "So let me tell you what I think."

"Any insight would be greatly appreciated," Monty said. "Thank you."

I didn't say anything because the pastrami on rye kept my mouth busy.

"Charon would never leave his post, but someone knew who and what he was collecting and wanted him out of the way. You find out who had access to that information, you find the Ferryman."

"Wait," I said after swallowing a bite. "To remove him we have to be talking major leagues here. Charon isn't a low-ranking soul transporter. He is one of the most powerful."

"*The* most powerful, so that should narrow it down for you," Ezra said. "I have to be off. Oh, one more thing, Charon is the *only* one missing. That should mean something too."

He grabbed his book, moved behind the counter, and disappeared into the back. Monty turned to stare at me.

"Really, you couldn't restrain yourself for a few minutes before attempting to devour that sarnie monstrosity?"

"He said eat," I said, preparing for another bite. "I don't argue with Death, so I ate. Try it, it's amazing."

Monty gave the sandwich a reluctant bite and he groaned in pleasure. My phone rang and I saw it was Ramirez.

"Where the hell have you been?" he yelled.

"You don't want to know. What's up?"

"We have a situation and you'd better get your asses here—yesterday," he said. "I'm sending you the address."

He hung up and I took another bite before getting up.

"If Ramirez is going to be summoning us every hour, we may need our own vehicle," Monty said as we left the deli. "Cecil may have something for us."

"Do you even know how to drive?" I asked. "I mean, in this part of the world, not backwards like you do 'across the pond.'"

"How hard could it be? We certainly can't have SuNaTran pick us up every bloody hour."

I looked down at my phone when it chirped and read the text from Ramirez.

"Shit, this is bad," I said. "We need to get back uptown now."

TWELVE

NEW YORK CITY taxis—or yellow kamikazes, as I call them—are the fastest way to travel above ground in the city. I hailed one. The driver, seemingly eager to test the tolerance of his brakes, screeched to stop a few feet away from us and beckoned us to enter his mobile torture chamber.

"What is Ramirez up in arms about now?" Monty said as he got in. "We just saw him."

"He has a few of your high caliber sorcerer friends at the museum," I said, sliding in next to him. "I thought sorcerers lived for centuries? Now all of the sudden they have the shelf life of yogurt. What's going on?"

"You're confusing sorcerers with mages and wizards," he said. "Sorcerers derive their power from the dark arts, which take a toll on the body. It's a real distinction you need to learn."

"I thought the magic would keep them alive," I said. "So, the dark arts…Not a fan?"

"I can access them, of course, but I choose not to," he said. "The cost is too high and the side effects aren't pleasant."

"Is it like those ads?" I asked. "'May cause baldness, blindness, rashes, nausea, diarrhea, and hemorrhoids'?"

"It's usually something a bit more final, like 'death after loss of limbs, unbearable stench, demonic attack, human sacrifice, and servitude to lower powers.'"

"How could anyone resist that?" I said. "What's the appeal?"

"It's the fastest route to power, takes less study, and requires little effort."

"Like magical CliffsNotes. They get to skip all the boring parts."

"Except those boring parts can keep you alive," he said, looking at the driver. "Do you intend on letting him know where we're going?"

"Hi, we need to get to MoMA ASAP," I said to the driver, who remained looking at me with a pleasant smile on his face. "Hello?"

"This is why I hate taxis," Monty said. "It's not even a proper color."

"Yes, I know," I said, pushing him aside. "All real taxis are black."

"Do you realize a London taxi driver takes two to four years to learn the knowledge? They have to *know* the city."

"We have the knowledge here too," I said. "We just happen to be a bit more sophisticated and call it by its American name—GPS."

I slid the small door of the partition to one side and looked at the driver's name: Khan, Amir—who, it seemed, was very happy on the day he took his license picture, judging from the immense smile. The same smile flashed at me when he had turned back to look at us.

"Where to, sir?" Amir asked with a thick South Asian accent.

"Amir, there's a twenty-dollar tip in it for you if you can get us to the Museum of Modern Art in under twenty minutes."

Amir gave me a blank stare for a few seconds.

"Where to, sir?" Amir asked again.

"Brilliant," Monty said, looking through the partition. "English probably isn't his second language, it seems more like a distant third or fourth."

"Amir," I said, and he smiled at me again, "11 West 53rd Street." I pointed at my watch and then showed him the twenty. "This is for you, extra, if you go fast— twenty minutes."

As if on cue, Amir turned on a small screen to the left of the steering wheel, which displayed a map, and our location in the city.

"Very good, sir," Amir said, and gave me a head wobble. "Twenty minutes."

He punched in the address I gave him and I turned to see Monty searching the seat for something.

"What did you lose?"

"Nothing, I'm looking for a bloody seatbelt."

"In a cab? In New York?" I asked, suppressing laughter and dread in equal measure. "You see those?"

I pointed to the straps that were bolted to the interior on both sides of the passenger area.

"Of course I see them. I'm not bloody blind."

"Those are the seatbelt substitutes. Grab one because English may not be his first language, but he understands the language of money."

I saw Amir smile as he executed a U-turn off the sidewalk, cutting off three cars and nearly hitting another as he swerved into traffic. He shot down 2nd Avenue and screeched onto the FDR Drive going uptown. The three-lane parkway named for our 32nd president was usually a traffic nightmare in the afternoon. I was about to suggest against it, when I saw him swerve around one vehicle and cut another off, all the while keeping a huge grin on his face. For Amir, the FDR had just become a giant slalom course.

"Bloody hell," Monty muttered, and bounced off one side of the cab. "Did you have to offer him extra money?"

"No, but then this wouldn't be as fun," I said and laughed at his expression of misery. "Stop being such a control freak. We'll get there in one piece."

"Oi!" Monty yelled. "Stop trying to kill us!"

Amir sped up in the center of the three lanes and then cut across sharply to the right, sliding into the far lane and then even farther into the service lane. I thought we were going to hit the dividing wall, when he shifted suddenly to the left and then back to the right to prevent another cab from passing him.

We veered off to the left, taking the exit on 61st Street as Amir swerved around the curve of the exit onto 2nd Avenue, and sped downtown. He ran through several yellow lights amidst a chorus of horns and screeching brakes. I marveled at how a squad of NYTF cruisers didn't appear behind us as we weaved through traffic, endangering life and limb.

"I thought—I thought yellow meant slow down?" Monty asked as we shot past an intersection and he bounced in his seat.

"That doesn't apply to taxis in New York," I said. "For cabs it means step on the gas and beat the red light."

Amir turned right on 53rd Street and headed across town. As he approached 5th Avenue, I felt Monty tense up next to me.

"Bollocks," he whispered as a fireball slammed into the cab, flipping us over.

THIRTEEN

SOMETHING VERY INTERESTING happens to your brain when faced with imminent death. Some people get hysterical. The majority of people get that deer-in-the-headlights reaction and don't know how to respond. I was somewhere between stunned and I need to get my ass moving. Everything seemed to slow down and a part of my brain kicked me into gear. Monty usually assisted with that part.

"Simon."

I heard my name muffled as if from a great distance. The cab was rotating slowly onto its roof as the fireball began melting the outside. Monty, who reacted faster than I did, was standing and moving with the impact of the strike.

One of his arms was extended while the other rested on the roof, making it appear he was doing a cartwheel. After about a second, I noticed the cab stopped rotating and we remained tilted on one side. The fear etched on Amir's face snapped me back to the present.

"Simon!" Monty yelled. "Get up there and get the driver out! I can't hold it like this all day."

Monty was sweating from the strain of keeping the cab in place and snuffing out the fireball that tried to melt us to slag.

"What?" I said. "Oh. Shit!"

I kicked in the partition and jumped into the driver's area, where a petrified Amir screamed at me in a language I didn't understand. Definitely in the hysterical group. I kicked open the passenger-side door and poked my head out. On the corner across from us, in front of the Rolex building, stood a man dressed in dark robes with black eldritch energy arcing around his body. He stood with his arms apart and screamed when he saw me looking at him.

"Monty, I think there's a sorcerer on the corner and he sounds really pissed," I said as I scrambled to the other door and kicked it open.

"Fancy that," Monty grunted. "What gave it away? The friendly fireball he launched at us or the fact that he's gathering negative energy to hurl this way?"

"I'm going to go with door number one. Fireballs are never friendly."

"Would you be so kind as to get your arse out of the taxi?"

I scrambled out of the cab and motioned for Amir to join me. He scampered out, still yelling at me in his native tongue. I held out the twenty and he gave me the 'are you an idiot?' look.

"Hey, deal's a deal," I said as the cab creaked behind us. "We may want to move now."

"You bloody bastards are insane," he said in perfect

English. "Stay away from me!"

Amir snatched the twenty from my hand and took off running in the direction of the museum. I looked down the block and saw NYTF squad cars blocking 5th Avenue and the entrance to MoMA. I moved away from the cab, keeping it between the angry sorcerer intent on testing my immortality and me.

It wasn't that I doubted being immortal. I had plenty of heavy hitters—gods, and other nearly omnipotent beings—tell me I was. It's just there was only one way to verify immortality. You have to die—and then come back. Or, even better, not die at all from something that should end you.

I had no problem with the 'coming back' part of the equation. The dying part, though, chafed. Mostly because I knew it involved pain. Then there was the other niggling thought that just wouldn't go away. Kali was an evil, conniving and vindictive goddess—on a good day. I wasn't just on her shit list; I was on the 'obliterate with extreme prejudice' list.

Her curse may have made me immortal, which I still didn't understand, but she could have twisted it with some condition like—'upon death, Simon will turn into a roach and live forever, even after being stomped on repeatedly.' Science has proven they're indestructible anyway. I just wouldn't want to be one.

So I tried to avoid dying as much as possible. Lately though, I wasn't having much luck staying out of potentially fatal situations.

I got about thirty feet away when the cab flew apart in several pieces. Monty stood in the wreckage, looking incredibly calm for someone who had just avoided incineration.

"Simon, you may want to step back," he said. "I'll deal with this *amateur*."

"You sure?" I asked. "I have the Ebonsoul."

He gave me a look and responded by spreading his arms and scattering the remains of the cab with a blast of air, clearing a path.

"No, then," I said, and stepped back even farther. I loaded the Grim Whisper and made sure I was out of the line of fire.

Monty walked across the street.

The Golden Circle mages is one of the oldest mage groups in existence. Monty didn't like to talk about them much and I hadn't been able to get a lot of information on them. Even The Hack came up with close to nothing. What he had found boiled down to a few things, They're old, secretive, powerful, and erased anyone who tried to find out more.

It was a lifetime membership and their idea of retirement involved your death. The fact that Monty had managed to leave alive made a few things clear: it was best not to piss him off, and he was probably one of the more powerful mages in the sect. Right now, the sorcerer across the street faced an angry Monty, and I backed up.

Black energy raced across the street and slammed into Monty. He extended one arm and absorbed the energy into him like a lightning rod.

"Fool, your death approaches," the sorcerer said in an unnatural voice that reverberated across the street and unleashed another barrage of dark lightning.

Monty stepped to the side and avoided the attack.

The lightning destroyed the concrete where it struck.

"Coward," Monty said. "Stop using surrogates and face me. If you dare."

I moved in closer to where Monty stood.

"Is that really a good idea?" I asked. "I mean, if this being can kidnap Charon and control dead sorcerers, maybe calling him out is not the best strategy?"

"It's the only way we'll know who we're facing," he said, "Besides it's not like you can die, and I'm an accomplished mage. How bad can it be?"

A red cloud surrounded the sorcerer, and I pulled Monty back.

"That doesn't look good," I said, taking more steps back.

"Agreed. That cloud reminds me of— shite, we need to run. Now!" he yelled and ran down the street in the direction of MoMA. I was right behind him, when I heard the thump. He turned and grabbed my wrist. The mala glowed white and threw up a shield. It launched us both down the street as the red cloud collided with it.

We landed unceremoniously in front of the museum and Ramirez's squad car. I looked around and saw the devastation. Everything the red cloud had touched was reduced to ash. I gave a silent thanks to Karma for the shield and dusted myself off as I stood. The sorcerer from the corner was gone. Monty stood up next to me and pointed. Down the street, two more sorcerers approached.

"I think I know who's controlling them," Monty said. "You aren't going to like it."

"There hasn't been anything about this day that

would go in the 'like' column. Tell me."

"That red cloud that disintegrates everything is the calling card of one being. If it's who I think it is, we may as well pack it in."

"What do you mean—pack it in?"

"As in drop this bloody mess and find a nice island to retire to for our last days," he said. "I'm a mage, not a god."

I heard real fear in his voice, which meant my fight-or-flight response kicked into flight on steroids.

I didn't want to ask, but I needed to know.

"Who is it?"

"It makes perfect sense now that I think of it. How did I not see it before?" Monty said as Ramirez approached our location.

Ramirez gave me a look. I shook my head, telling him to leave it alone.

"Monty," I said, "who's the bad guy trying to kill us?"

He snapped back and focused on me.

"Not just us. He wants to end *everything*. Always has."

"Oh, now I don't feel so bad—who, Monty?"

"Chaos."

FOURTEEN

"CHAOS, AS IN the force of chaos?" I asked. "You mean, like the opposite of order?"

"No. Chaos, as in the god. That red cloud is called a chaotic mist. No one else does that. It requires a living sacrifice."

"I don't like him already," I said. "So we're talking what—major leagues here?"

"If he's involved, he somehow stopped Charon and is enthralling recently dead sorcerers to do…well, whatever it is he's doing," Monty answered. "Yes, I would say several leagues above whatever you or I can deal with."

"So just to be clear, when you say living sacrifice, you mean the sorcerer…?"

"Is the catalyst for the mist—yes."

"Maybe it's a copycat god, someone trying to make a name for him or herself?" I said, hoping against hope.

"No," he said. "No one would dare mimic Chaos. Not if they wanted to remain breathing."

His words hit me with a sense of finality that rocked me to my core. I felt my stomach do a somersault.

"I'm calling her," I said. "This is beyond the both of us."

"Chaos who?" Ramirez asked, looking at us. "What is he talking about? Oh and maybe we want to stop them?"

He pointed at the advancing sorcerers.

"What about the rune of negation?" I asked. "Can we use it here?"

Ramirez shook his head.

"Too dangerous in an open area like this," he said. "If we unleash it, it could negate *everything* in a five-hundred yard radius. At least that's what they told me. That's why I called you two."

"That's technically correct," Monty answered. "Do you have it here?"

Ramirez nodded. "It's in the case in my car."

"What was the Golden Circle thinking when they made that thing?" I said, looking at Monty. "It sounds like a magical nuke."

"We were thinking of ending the war," he said. "It wasn't supposed to be used after the war."

He pulled me back, away from Ramirez, who remained where he stood, his gaze fixed on the approaching sorcerers.

"Make sure there are no civilians within the cordon," Ramirez said into his shoulder radio. "Tell me the museum has been evacuated."

"Affirmative, sir," a voice said. "No civilians are inside the cordon. Some of the men would prefer to be outside with them."

"And I would like to be sitting by the beach in Miami," Ramirez barked. "But I'm here stuck with all of you. Suck it up and put on your big-boy pants."

"You have ten seconds, right?" Monty asked, grabbing my attention when we were some distance from Ramirez.

"On the outside," I said. "I haven't actually timed it. Plus time itself gets twisted when I use it so I don't really know how long it is."

"In five years you haven't measured how long it lasts?" he asked and rolled his eyes. "Why do I punish myself this way?"

"In five years—this will be the fourth time I use it," I shot back quickly. "You remember that last time I had to use it?"

He held up his hand. "Forget I asked," he said. "I will time it this time and if you survive we will know how long."

"What do you mean if I survive?"

"I'm going to release the negation rune and you're going to take it to them," he said, looking at the sorcerers. "You will have ten seconds before we are all reduced to... well, there won't be anything *to* reduce if you fail."

"Why can't you just cast it at them?"

"It's not a spell you can cast," he said. "It has to be placed. It was one of the constraints placed on its creation. It must remain in a fixed location and then activated."

"So throw it at them," I said. "This is probably one of your worst ideas."

"Worse than throwing a rune capable of nullifying

everything around it and hoping they will remain in place while it destroys them?"

"When you put it like that—"

"It doesn't matter," he said, heading to the car and pulling out the case holding the rune. "The rune needs to be placed on a target to be effective."

"Guys…"Ramirez said. "If you're going to do something, now would be a good time."

The sorcerers approached the museum entrance. One remained at the door and the other was about to enter.

"Why are they even here?" I asked. "Is Chaos a big art-lover?"

"I'm giving you twenty seconds. Put the rune around that sorcerer's neck" —he pointed at the one guarding the entrance—"and get back to me in that time."

"Worst-case scenario?" I asked, not really wanting the answer.

"You take too long—we all die."

"But this rune is magic, so I should be immune."

"The catalyst is magic, but the effect is real. Everything is in a state of entropy and—you know what? Here's the condensed version. You take too long, you'll be erased along with everything around you. That bloody clear enough?"

"Crystal," I said, looking at the rune. "Just tell me when."

He took the rune and held the golden disc. A thin chain was looped on either side of it, which allowed it to be hung or attached to a target. Monty closed his eyes and focused. Nothing happened for a few seconds and then it exploded in light, blinding me for a split second. I blinked but had to look away, the light was so intense. It reminded me of a miniature sun sitting there.

"Now, Simon!" he yelled.

I placed my right hand on my left, making sure to touch the two points of the endless knot with my thumb and index fingers, and focused. White light raced from each end and connected at the center and then time stopped. I took the disc from Monty and sprinted the half-block to the sorcerers.

Everything around me was slightly out of focus. Panting with my heart hammering against my chest, I made it to the sorcerer guarding the door and placed the rune around his neck. I noticed movement in my peripheral vision and used a second to look in the museum but saw nothing. I turned and dashed back, realizing I was already running out of time.

I was about halfway back to Monty when the world erupted behind me.

FIFTEEN

THERE WAS A loud crack followed by a deep bass thump that punched my lower abdomen and I knew the negation rune had started. I looked at the mark and the white light that filled it had dimmed and was disappearing.

I pressed the center orb of the mala and felt the shield come up around me as everything snapped back into focus and a wave of energy launched me past a surprised Monty. I bounced on the street and rolled for several feet before I was able to look back. Monty caught up with me as I was getting to my feet. He was frozen midstride. His hands gave off a golden glow and he was shouting something at me. Ramirez was midair as he dived behind his car. The sorcerer at the door was being annihilated by the negation rune as the chaotic mist surrounded him.

The world had gone out of focus again. I looked down at my mark but it was dim, which only meant one thing. She was coming.

"Goddammit, I told him she would show up," I said to no one in particular.

A burning sensation tore through my left hand and made me gasp in pain. I looked down at the mark and saw it had turned a deep red. The usual citrusy aroma of lotus flowers and wet earth was replaced with a rancid smell. That same odor filled the nightmare emergency scenario every New Yorker dreads—stepping inside a public bathroom. They look promising from the outside, but once you take one step in, your sense of smell is strangled, thrown to the ground, and stomped on until your eyes water and your nose begs for mercy. If you manage to last more than ten seconds, permanent olfactory damage results in you never smelling the world the same way again.

"This looks promising," a voice said behind me—a male voice. "Hello, Detective."

I reached for the Ebonsoul before turning and found myself airborne. I landed about ten feet away with no sword and a broken arm. My vision began tunneling in when the pain cascaded over me and yanked me back. Someone was grinding a boot into the break.

He wore a black trench coat and looked like he shopped in the same places Ken frequented. It was black with an undertone of black and black accents. His hair was cut in a screaming eagle and his posture reminded me of ex-military. Around his neck hung an ornate amulet made of gold. It was covered in runes. The center was blank and it looked like a piece was missing.

The eyes gave it away. They glowed a deep blue and

pulsed as he took in the scene. It was a good clue I wasn't dealing with a human. I know, my powers of perception astounded even me.

"Who—what—the hell are you?" I grunted through the pain. "Where's Karma and what's with all the black?"

"Simon Strong," he said, looking at me, "I heard you can't die and are calling you the chosen of Kali, but we both know that's not true."

"She cursed me," I said. "There was no 'choosing.' She wants me to suffer."

He twirled the Ebonsoul on one finger as he spoke. "Here in this place" —he spread his arms wide—"you are very, very mortal."

He buried the Ebonsoul in my leg. I screamed. He laughed.

"You're interfering in things way beyond your comprehension," he said calmly once my screams subsided.

"Enlighten me," I said through the throbbing in my leg. I was losing a lot of blood and felt lightheaded.

"No, it doesn't concern you—not your circus, not your monkeys," he said with a smile. "Besides, you're being used. Wake up before you end up dead."

"Some people disagree," I said. "Some people feel you need to be stopped. Where's Charon?"

He chuckled. "Now *that* would be cheating, Detective," he said. "Time to go." He touched the amulet. "I have what I need, and you have—well, you have a life-threatening wound in your leg. If I were you, I'd get that looked at."

He placed a foot on the hilt of the Ebonsoul and

stepped down. I screamed again.

"You bastard," I gasped when the pain subsided. "I'll stop you."

He removed his foot and crouched down next to me.

"Pathetic. It's not surprising you never amounted to much," he said and laughed again. "There's just so little potential. That ring a bell?"

The words hurt more than the sword buried in my leg. They were the words burned into my memory when they discharged me. Those same words were used when they had judged me and deemed me unfit for service.

"Furgk...you," I slurred and pulled the Ebonsoul out of my leg. "You...you don't know me."

He shook his head. "*That* may have been a mistake. Looks like you've lost a bit of blood," he said and grabbed my hand. My mark had gone dark. "Time for you to go, too. By the way, that was an impressive move with the negation rune. You managed to take out both of my sorcerers and most of the atrium. If it had been a battle rune, it would've done some serious damage."

"Sorry I missed you...Chaos."

Blackness was creeping in from the edges of my vision.

He stood and gave me a sweeping bow. "I'm your huckleberry," he said and grew serious. "Stay out of my affairs, Strong. Or next time I bury your butter knife in your chest."

I pulled out Grim Whisper and fired, but he was already gone. Everything snapped back into focus and I passed out.

SIXTEEN

WHEN I OPENED my eyes, the first thing I saw was Monty's face. His expression told me all I needed to know. I looked as bad as I felt. Never big on emotion, he had two settings—mildly annoyed and white-hot rage. This was one of those rare moments I saw genuine concern. That expression scared me more than Chaos.

"Still alive," I whispered and regretted speaking immediately. Everything hurt, even my hair. "Although I think death would feel better right about now."

"You look like shite," he said. "What bloody happened?"

"Used the rune like you said," I said, narrowing my eyes at him, "It didn't have twenty seconds on it—closer to *ten*, Tristan."

"You're upset. I'm sorry, Simon, I thought I gave you enough time—evidently not."

"It was Chaos," I said and groaned. "He somehow pulled a Karma and stepped in while I was in the stasis."

"He attacked you during?"

"*Attack* is a strong word, more like toyed with," I replied, and groaned as I shifted off my leg. "We can't face him. He is off-the-charts powerful."

I tried to move again and my body screamed at me. I looked across the street and saw the wreckage from the negation rune. The two sorcerers were nowhere to be found.

"Shit, the rune did that?" And the sorcerers?"

Monty nodded, his face grim. "They're gone," he said. "The mist consumed them."

The front of the museum was obliterated. It looked like someone had used an enormous knife and sliced off a large chunk. Most of the sidewalk and street in front of MoMA was missing. Some of the NYTF squad cars that formed the cordon near the entrance were sheared cleanly in half. The others inside the cordon were gone.

"That rune should never have been created," he whispered. "It made the Golden Circle a destroyer of worlds. We became death."

"Monty, Oppenheimer is a little dark, even for you," I said with a tight smile as he looked me over. "How bad?"

He examined the extent of the damage as Ramirez approached us from across the street.

"The arm will need to be reset before it heals completely," he said as he prodded. "The wound in your leg looks like it's healing, but judging from your symptoms you're going through a class-two hemorrhage. We need a hospital."

"Ambulances are on the way," Ramirez said over the squawk of his shoulder radio. "What just happened? One second I'm standing next to you two, the next you're over here looking like you've been chewed up and spit out."

"Chaos happened." I groaned and sat up. I was feeling slightly better.

"Goddamn right it's chaos. Do you see the museum?" Ramirez asked. "And how am I supposed to explain my missing squad cars? You need to get out of here before the brass shows up. I have enough to deal with."

"Something is missing from the museum," I said.

"Oh, funny, you're a comedian all of a sudden," Ramirez answered.

"I'm serious, something is gone," I said.

I didn't want to explain that a god with some insane agenda just stole something from the museum. He would probably think I was delirious.

"Yeah, the entire façade and most of the atrium is missing. Is he delirious?" Ramirez said, looking at Monty.

"No, inside," I said as the ground tilted at a sharp angle. "From the inside. Something was taken."

"It's possible the sorcerers were a diversion for a theft," Monty said, holding me still. "You may want to get an inventory of what was on exhibit and what's gone."

"You're kidding, right?" Ramirez said, the sarcasm dripping from his words. "It's going to take forever to sift through all of this...this disaster. Remind me to thank you both later—especially you, Strong."

"Did you secure the rune?" Monty asked. "You need to get that in a vault."

"Of course I secured it. Are you saying *it* was responsible for all this damage? Not him?" Ramirez said, pointing at me.

"Well, a combination of both actually," Monty replied.

"We live to slerve," I said, my tongue thick. "Do we send you an invoice for this or should we discuss that later?"

"Get me an inventory of everything that was on the affected floors," Ramirez said into his radio as he looked daggers at me and gave me the finger. "That's my answer to your invoice."

"I'm guessing that's a no," I answered, looking at Monty. "Is that a no?"

"He looks like shit," Ramirez said to Monty. "Get him out of my face and out of my scene as soon as the first bus shows up." He walked off, giving more orders as first responders started arriving.

"Ambulances will take an eternity to get here. I'm calling Cecil," Monty said and pulled out his phone. "Hold still, Simon."

"I am still, it's the world that's moving sideways. Is Robert going to get here faster than the carrots in the field?"

"What? Stop talking. You've lost too much blood," he said as my vision tunneled in and I laid my head on the cool pavement and closed my eyes. The sirens echoed through the early evening as the ambulances approached.

"We can't fight him, Monty," I said as the fog in my

brain started to clear. "Time to go on vacay. Far, far away."

"Cecil, send Robert," Monty said, ignoring me. "Bloody now... Track my location... Good."

"He has Charon," I said. "Has him hidden."

"Did he tell you where? What did he say exactly? Did he give you any idea what he took from the museum?"

"He said it would be cheating if he told me. Bastard broke my arm and disarmed me in one move. I didn't even see it coming."

"Did he give you any idea what he took?"

"No. He just said he had what he came for. It didn't sound good for us, Monty."

"I'm taking you to Haven," he said. "The hospitals wouldn't know what to do with you. Roxanne is expecting us."

"Heaven? You think the big guy would let me in?"

"Don't be daft, I said Haven not Heaven, and no, you are most likely on the 'Do Not Admit' list."

The black Phantom approached seconds later, gliding to our position and rolling to a stop. Robert stepped out as the passenger doors opened. He picked me up gently from the ground with Monty instructing him about my mangled arm and the wound in my leg. He nodded as he placed me in the rear and strapped me in.

"Bobby, you're good people," I said as he tightened the seatbelt. "Monty, make sure he gets a raise."

"I'm quite adequately compensated, Mr. Strong," Robert answered, "but thank you for the sentiment."

"Simon, Bobby— it's Simon."

"Yes, Mr. Strong, sir," he replied and got behind the

wheel.

Monty sat next to me with a concerned look on his face.

"Haven, Robert, with haste," he said.

Robert pulled away and sped down Fifth Avenue for several blocks, clearing the cordon before turning east.

"Monty, I'll be fine, I'm feeling better already," I said. "My body will handle this just fine."

It was true, the fog had lifted, and my thoughts were getting clearer by the second.

"What? Oh, I'm not thinking about you," he said, distracted. "I'm wondering why he didn't just kill you."

"Excuse me?"

"If he perceived you as a threat, why not just remove you from the board? He had ample opportunity."

"Your concern for my well-being is overwhelming. Stop now before I tear up."

"I'm not saying he *should* have killed you," he replied. "I'm wondering why he didn't. You were vulnerable and he had the means to do so. He chose to stab your leg and break your arm. It doesn't fit…unless…"

"Unless?"

"We're here," he said. "Roxanne will have to break that arm again. I trust you're ready?"

"Unless what?" I asked, trying to press him.

He always deflected when he didn't want to share something unpleasant. We pulled into an ambulance bay and several medical orderlies waited outside with a gurney. Two of them hoisted me up, placed me in it, and began strapping me down.

"Robert, thank you for your service," Monty said. "Please inform Cecil we will be looking for a personal vehicle. Can you have him give me a call when you return?"

Robert tipped his hat and pressed the button to close the Phantom's doors. "Will do, sir," he said and pulled off.

"I won't be getting into any vehicle if you're driving, Monty," I said as they pushed me inside. "Unless it's a M1 Abrams."

"Duly noted," he said. "By the way, the stasis lasted ten seconds, exactly."

"It felt a lot longer, especially when Chaos was 'visiting' me."

"That poses several questions. He was in the vicinity. Your use of the mark could've alerted him to your presence."

"Karma said something like that," I answered in between the bounces as they wheeled me in. "That I should be careful because the mark would attract those outside of time."

"That doesn't explain how he managed to enter the stasis and why didn't Karma show?"

"Still wondering that myself."

"It could be Kali created the mark as a beacon to alert other beings powerful enough to destroy you every time you used it," he said. "It's one theory."

"Sounds like her. She gets rid of me and keeps her hands clean."

"Hello, Tristan," a husky female voice said, the sound filling the hall. "What happened?"

"Roxanne," he said, giving her a short nod and then gesturing at me and almost gushing. "The usual— Simon."

I broke out in my best rendition of The Police's famous song and threatened to shatter all of the glass in proximity with my melodious voice.

"That never gets old, Simon," she said with a wince. "If the band could hear your horrific rendition, I'm sure they would ask you to stop. Or beg me to rip out your vocal chords. Most likely the latter."

"Hello, Roxy, how are you?" I said with a forced smile.

"I've been better," she said. She looked me over and gave Monty a sidelong glance. "As have you. Are you going around pissing off werewolves again?"

"Monty missed you. I had to get hurt just so he could come see you."

"How kind of you," she said and smiled. "How have you been, Tristan?"

She was a tall, slim brunette with deep green eyes you could get lost in. Tristan never admitted his feelings for her, but I knew him well enough to see the signs. I never brought it up because the idea of being barbequed wasn't appealing and he had a tendency to get all fire-magey when I brought her up.

"I've been meaning to come by... I—we've— just been swamped with cases," he said, nonplussed. His calm demeanor suddenly on shaky ground, I shook my head and suppressed a laugh.

She placed a hand on his wrist and smiled at him. I swear he blushed.

"Can you tell me what happened?" she asked. "I can see the break, which will need to be broken and reset, and the wound, which is almost healed. How did this occur?"

Monty explained everything as he wheeled me into an operating room. The runes on the threshold flared as we walked by and sterilized us.

Haven was the primary supernatural medical facility in the city, if not the entire East Coast. Located on 1st Avenue between 37th and 38th Streets, the massive facility was part hospital and part detention center. Some of the most dangerous supernaturals were held there.

Roxanne DeMarco was one of the directors of the facility. She oversaw both the medical and detention centers and led the general pathology department. She did her job with a ruthless efficiency. I'd seen her take down creatures twice her size without breaking a sweat. She was also the only sorceress Monty respected as a peer. Actually, she was the only sorceress he respected —period.

After Kali cursed me, he brought me to her when he couldn't find an answer. Between the both of them, they figured out what the mark did.

"So you've upgraded to pissing off gods now?" she said.

"It wasn't intentional; besides, he seemed cranky when we met," I said.

"You have that effect on people," Monty answered and then paused. He looked sharply at Roxanne, who nodded. "Did you feel that?"

"Is it a disturbance in the energy that connects us all?" I asked. "You know a disturbance in the—"

"Don't," he said, "or I swear I will hit you hard enough to cause catastrophic damage."

"It came from the detention center," Roxanne said.

"Are the security measures in place?" Monty asked.

"Always. I'll take care of Simon. Can you go take a look?" This won't take long and I'll be there shortly."

Monty gave us a curt nod and walked off.

"You didn't have to get rid of him," I said. "You know how he feels about you, right?"

"I'm concerned about him. He won't listen to me, but he will listen to you."

"What do you mean?"

"Every mage has an energy signature. It's as unique as our fingerprints."

"Are you saying there's something wrong with his? Are you seeing something?"

"That's exactly it. I'm not seeing it."

"Maybe he's in stealth mode—you know, masking it so he can't be traced."

"He can't mask it from me," she said with a small smile and then grew serious. "Every part of him is open to me."

"Yeah, okay, thanks—TMI," I said. "So his signature is fuzzy? You have to explain this masking to me."

"That's just it. Even masked I should still be able to see some trace of it."

"What are you saying?"

"I don't sense an energy signature from him—nothing. It's like he doesn't exist."

"Are you telling me that's not Monty?"

"No, what I'm saying is that something's off—" she started and then stopped.

That's when I felt the rumbling.

"Those security measures you were talking about —?" I started.

"Just fell," she said, her face grim. "Hold on while I set this. On three. Ready?"

I nodded and braced for the pain.

"One," she said, and broke my arm—again.

"Goddammit!" I screamed as the pain shot up my arm and lodged itself in my brain like an ice pick. "What happened to 'on three'?"

"I heard the pain is less if it's a surprise," she said with a smile. "Plus we're a little short on time."

"That's a bullshit rumor and you know it," I snapped.

"I know," she said, looking down at her watch. "You should be healed soon."

It was a good thing I was strapped down in the gurney, because in that moment I really wanted to punch her in the head. Then I remembered that she was probably as powerful as Monty so I rethought the strategy. After a few seconds, she undid the straps.

"What are you doing?" I asked.

"How do you feel? Are you armed?"

I flexed the fingers of my recently mangled arm. The pain was minimal. I had full mobility and some stiffness.

"Feels almost normal, just a little stiff," I said.

"Good, do you have your weapons?" Her voice sounded calm but there was an urgency in the tone.

Yes, but why would I need—?"

"Because the detention center was just breached and the creature coming this way is currently impervious to my ability."

"Excuse me? What creature?"

The crashing that filled the room kicked my body

into fight-or-flight mode, heavy on the flight. It sounded like the medical facility was being shredded in half. I ran out to the hallway and saw Monty in the distance come running around the corner. His shirt was torn off in places and it looked like he was bleeding from several cuts on his face.

Behind him, moving almost as fast but twice as large, was something my brain couldn't or didn't accept. It was a large man in what looked like a hospital gown. He was covered in scars and muscle and looked enraged.

"Strong!" the creature yelled. "Time to die!"

It ripped off the doors and tossed them to one side as it pounded its huge fists into the walls, leaving large craters.

"What the hell is that?" I asked in disbelief. "Why is he calling *my* name?"

"That would be the creature I was talking about," she said as calmly as if she were giving me the time of day. "It would seem he's enthralled."

"Simon!" Monty yelled. "Run!"

SEVENTEEN

FOR THE BRIEFEST of moments, I considered pulling out the Ebonsoul, then realized that Monty was running *away* from the thing.

I ran down the hallway and burst through a set of double doors with Monty behind me and the escapee from every nightmare I've ever had not far behind him.

"We need to get outside, Simon!" he yelled as we rushed into the stairwell and ran down the stairs.

I slammed open the door leading to the garage, when a tremendous crash filled the stairs. Judging from the rubble, it looked like it decided to leap from the top floor. The stairwell was full of debris, completely burying the creature.

"What the hell was that thing?" I said as I caught my breath and approached the stairwell. "And why was it calling *my* name when it was chasing *you*?"

"Stay away from the doorway," Monty said as he began inscribing runes into the doorframe. "That is an ogre, and I don't think that little fall is going to stop it."

"Little fall? It just destroyed an entire ten floors of stairwell."

"Ogres aren't known for stopping. They're single-minded creatures of destruction. Almost impossible to control, hard to defeat, and resistant to most forms of magic."

"Sounds like a perfect weapon," I said, stepping back from the glowing designs he inscribed.

"That's what they were during the war, but I haven't seen one since then," he said. "Most of them went into hiding or real estate."

"Real estate?" "I said. "Ogres owning property?"

Monty nodded as he added runes to the ground in front of the door and then backed up.

"Ogres are shrewd when it comes to lairs and caves. They just upgraded to buildings. They are highly intelligent, contrary to their depiction in fiction," he said.

"Roxanne said it was enthralled. Did she mean like the sorcerers?" I said. "She said her ability wouldn't work on it."

Monty nodded. "Seems this is Chaos again—where did he get an ogre? Why was it screaming your name? We're obviously missing something."

"We need to find Charon. This situation is getting out of control," I said. "I hope those are ogre-stopping runes?"

"I don't know any 'ogre stopping' runes. Those are designed to keep it in place in case it tries to escape the stairwell. I'll call Roxanne and they can get a containment unit down here to retrieve it."

I exhaled, letting out the breath I didn't know I had

been holding as we walked up the ramp to the exit. I looked back over my shoulder a few times to make sure it remained trapped.

"So it's stuck there?" I asked. "The runes will hold it?"

The ogre roared and broke the wall next to the stairwell entrance. It peered through the gaping hole and focused on me. It knocked down more of the wall and stepped through, shaking off dust and debris.

"Unless of course it decides to just go through the wall adjacent to the runes I just placed," he said. "Seems this one is quite intelligent, or being guided."

We backpedaled up the ramp. I pulled out the Ebonsoul.

"Monty, we can't take that thing outside," I said. "It's too dangerous. What if it decides to attack others?"

He rubbed his chin. "There is that possibility. What do you propose?"

"We stop it here," I said, "before it gets outside."

"Just the two of us?"

"Sure, we can do it."

"Simon, I applaud your confidence, misguided as it may be, but *that* is an ogre. I can't use all of my magic."

"Can it die?" I asked.

"Well, of course it can die—"

"Then we need to stop it. What, are you scared?"

He nodded. "Shitless, because my brain operates with common sense, unlike yours."

The ogre began climbing up the ramp.

"Common sense isn't going to stop that thing. Can you use your black-hole spell again?"

"An entropy spell—any spell—would be too

dangerous. It might get deflected and hit you," he said. "This one is going to require a hands-on approach."

"Wonderful," I said as I began walking down the ramp.

With each step, the voice in my head, which sounded eerily like Monty, screamed at me to run in the opposite direction. It's a good thing I had practice rarely listening to that voice.

"Strong, I'm going to kill you and then chew on your bones," the ogre said with a snarl. "Then I'm going to kill your little magic fairy friend."

A chuckle escaped me. The alternative was I wet my pants.

"Are you calling Monty a fairy?" I asked. "He prefers magical fairy being. He's very proper, being English and all."

"Bloody hells, Simon, are you trying to anger it further?" Monty hissed at me. "I truly hope you were paying attention during your last lesson with Master Yat."

"Yes," I said and started laughing. The ogre's face twisted into a grimace and it screamed, charging at me.

Master Yat was our martial arts teacher and one of the few people who knew about my 'affliction,' as he called it. He was a slight man of Asian ancestry and indeterminate age. His unassuming stature hid a ferocious fighter. According to Monty, Master Yat was a dangerous ally during the war. He was known for devastating attacks with his bamboo staff.

As far as I knew, he had no magical ability except that he was somehow like me—immune to the effects of magic. This pissed off Monty to no end. That alone made the torture sessions he called class worth it.

The last lesson was still fresh in my mind.

"When faced with an opponent larger, stronger, and more powerful than yourself, what do you do?" he asked me.

"Run and hide and let Monty deal with it?" I said. "I mean—take cover until Monty can neutralize the threat."

"And if Tristan is down or hurt? What then?"

"He never gets hurt and he doesn't know how to get down—he's English. In that case, I scoop up Monty and then run and hide?"

No matter how fast I tried to move, his bamboo staff would catch me. The *thwack* reverberated across the dojo we trained in as I tried my best to stand still and revel in the sensation of sudden and instant pain.

"Wrong," he said. "You stay and fight."

"You just said the opponent was larger, stronger, and more powerful. How am I supposed to fight something like that?"

"Each of those attributes can be turned to your advantage if you know how."

"Isn't that why we're here?"

Another whack with the staff.

"No one likes a smartass. Practice the evasion drill again."

I used that same drill now.

The ogre leaped up the ramp, a bundle of muscle and rage. Monty peeled off to the side, his hands glowing. One of the problems with being extra-large, like an ogre, is that fighting in a garage limits your mobility and headroom. It had to remain crouched as it closed on me. This removed its height advantage.

It dived forward and swiped at me.

I rolled to the side and buried the Ebonsoul in its side, slicing as I ran past. The scream threatened to deafen me as I jumped to the side and narrowly avoided a kick. Monty released two deep red orbs. They hit the ogre and sank into the floor.

"Your magic is useless against me, sorcerer," it said as it roared again. It ignored Monty and focused on me.

Monty's jaw flexed as he narrowed his eyes.

"With 'fairy' he might've let you go with just some pain," I said, shaking my head, "but then you had to go and call him a sorcerer. Bad move."

The ogre looked at me with a hint of confusion before attacking again. I fell on my back and under another swipe and kicked up with my feet, connecting with its head. It brought a fist down, and I managed to block with the Ebonsoul at the last second. I felt the air escape my lungs in a whoosh as it used its other hand to whack me down the ramp. I bounced for a few feet before coming to a stop.

The ogre laughed as it stepped toward me. Monty stepped in front of me, his hands glowing red.

"Out of my way, sorcerer. I'll crush you after I'm done with him," it said.

"No, you're done now," Monty whispered.

"Your magic can't touch me."

"I don't need it to," Monty said and unleashed the orbs in his hands. "I only need a focus."

The orbs rushed at the ogre, who reflexively lifted his hands to cover his face. The asphalt under the ogre went from solid to semi-liquid, causing it to sink in place. It reminded me of a dinosaur falling into a tar pit.

The orbs homed in on the Ebonsoul, which I had left buried in the ogre's hand when I blocked his last attack. They hit the hilt with a crack and funneled down the blade and into the body of the ogre, who looked up at us with a mixture of rage, confusion, and fear.

"What have you done?" it roared at us. "I'll kill you, sorcerer!"

"I am not a bloody sorcerer!" Monty yelled. "That was the last mistake you made."

The ogre placed its hands on either side of the asphalt pool and tried to climb out. Monty placed his hands together in the form of prayer and spread them forcefully.

The magic inside the body of the ogre exploded outward, disintegrating everything from the waist up. Ogre chunks flew everywhere—many of them landing on me.

"Would a warning have been too much?" I asked as I removed large pieces of ogre from my jacket.

I walked over to retrieve the Ebonsoul, which was covered in ogre goo.

"I was a little preoccupied with not getting crushed, eviscerated, and gnawed on," he said. "I'd better call Roxanne to get this mess."

"I notice none of the ogre bits landed on you. How'd you manage that?"

"Practice." He gave me a smile as he pulled out his phone. "Let me put this on speaker while I secure the area. Ogre remains can be toxic."

"Now you tell me," I muttered, removing more of the goo.

He handed me the phone as he cast a spell over the area. The line rang three times before connecting, and I put it on speakerphone.

"Hello," Roxanne said. "Tristan?"

"Roxanne," Monty said, "we're in the garage with ogre everywhere. I'm containing as much as I can, but you'll need a clean-up crew down here."

Another voice came on the line.

"You two defeated an ogre? I'm impressed. I should've sent two."

It was Chaos.

Monty stopped moving and looked at the phone.

"What do you want?" Monty said with barely contained rage.

"What I've always wanted," Chaos said with a laugh just this side of deranged. "The end of everything."

"The ogre was a diversion?" I said. "Are you kidding me?"

"If you harm her…" Monty said as he formed his hands into fists, waves of heat coming off his body.

"No, I need this sorceress alive. At least for now."

"You need to let her go—now," Monty answered.

"I can tell you're upset, so I won't take up too much of your time, Tristan. Try to understand, this isn't personal."

"It is now," Monty whispered. "Let her go and I promise to kill you quickly."

"Kill me?" Chaos said and laughed. "Strong, you might want to help your mage friend understand what he's up against before he gets you both killed."

"I will find you and end you," Monty said.

"Not if I end you first," Chaos said and hung up.

EIGHTEEN

WE FOUND THE nearest stairwell and ran up. I didn't try to reason with Monty in his current state. Right now, I was just running damage control and hoped he didn't blow the hospital to tiny little pieces.

When we reached the tenth floor, we stopped in the stairwell.

"Monty, there may be another ogre in there, for all we know," I said. "It's not like the last one was a cakewalk. Let's get backup."

"He has Roxanne. You're the only backup I need, Simon. Are you coming?"

He grabbed the door handle and pulled. I drew Grim Whisper and aimed down the hallway, at least what used to be the hallway.

"What the hell?" I said. "Where's the rest of it?"

Most of the hallway was gone. It looked like someone had taken a large chunk out of the building, then I realized it looked familiar.

"Do you think he has a negation rune?" I asked as

the words chilled me to the core. "Because this looks a lot like MoMA."

"If he does, we're in the deepest shite conceivable," Monty said, as he stepped around the rubble and stopped. "We need to go. She won't be here."

The air around him was charged with energy. He stood rigid with anger as he took in the scene of destruction. I chose my next words carefully.

"Fighting an angry ogre works up an appetite," I said slowly. "Let's swing by Polanco's and then home so I can clean off the ogre bits from my clothes and you can change."

For several seconds he stood unimaginably still and looked at the hallway. I reached over and placed a hand on his shoulder.

"Monty, we will get her back, I swear," I whispered, pulling him gently, "but we need to find out why he needs sorcerers. Let's call Ramirez and find out what he took from the museum. It's our best lead."

He nodded. "You grab some Polanco's and then head to the office," he said. "I need to prepare some countermeasures. If we are going up against a god, we need to be ready."

I couldn't imagine what kind of countermeasures he would take to face a god. It was in moments like these that I was glad Monty was on my side.

"Sounds like a plan," I said. "Robert, then?"

"No. I'll take a cab. I need to get us a proper mode of transport."

I pulled out my phone and pressed the button for SuNaTran. They would send a car to my location.

"I have a car coming. Are you sure you don't want a

ride?" I could drop you off."

"No, thank you. It will be night soon. You should head to the Moscow just in case Georgianna gets any more 'visitors.' I'm sure your vampire will be paying you a visit. Especially after today. I'll meet you there in an hour."

"And you will be…? In case I need to contact you?" I asked. I didn't like the idea of him wandering the city in a simmering fury. It was the kind of thing that ended up on the news—*Crater swallows several midtown buildings, cause unknown. Witnesses report an angry mage leaving the scene.*

"I'm going to Cecil's to get us a vehicle. We can't be dependent on SuNaTran if we need to be mobile."

"Fine," I said. I would call Cecil and give him a heads-up about Monty's state of mind. It was another way to keep an eye on him. "Whatever you do, don't let Cecil try and give you any kind of Volkswagen. Especially not a bug. I'm particular to the color blue, however."

"Any other requests?" he said as he hailed a cab.

"Yes, try not to incinerate the city on the way to Cecil's. It would make things awkward."

"Duly noted," he said and got in the cab. "See you in an hour."

"One hour," I said and watched him take off.

I let him go because I knew he needed to vent, and as close as we were, he preferred to do his venting alone. Also, I didn't want an angry mage around jittery vampires, and he was right, I had a feeling Michiko would be paying me a visit tonight.

I headed over to Polanco's, which was about a block

away from the Moscow. It served the best Dominican food on the planet. I picked up an order of their sautéed beef with white rice and beans. I ordered the Monty special, which the owner, Samuel, called 'el Monte'—a salad so good I almost considered going vegan.

I looked out the window and across the street and saw two men enter the meat market. They looked like the vamps I had fought at the blood bank.

I grabbed my order and crossed the street. I popped into the Randy Rump, an old-style butcher shop. Behind the counter stood a large man with long gray hair that was pulled back in a ponytail. He wore an apron over a T-shirt and jeans. His massive arms, which were easily the size of my legs, were covered with thick hair.

"We're about to close up," he said as he put choice cuts of meat away in the freezer in the back. "What do you need?"

The two men tried their best to look normal—which is always a giveaway, especially with hit— I mean, *Resolution Teams*. The black suits and glasses didn't help, either.

"They were here before me; I'll wait," I said to the butcher as I gestured at the two. I turned away from them but kept a bead on their location using the reflection in the display case in front of me.

I let my hand rest on the hilt of the Ebonsoul, when a familiar scent wafted past my nose. I stepped to the door and looked up at the evening sky. A fat yellow moon began its ascent in the night sky, and I smiled.

If my guess was right, these two were in for a world

of pain. Occasionally, even after the formation of the Dark Council, vampires hunted other supernatural species. They considered themselves the apex predator and eliminated any perceived threats to their territory. The two suits were a Resolution Team, but not for Georgianna—they were here for the butcher. And they weren't too bright.

I had only smelled that odor— a mix between wet dog and musk—once in my life. I shuddered when I remembered the reason. Once was enough.

One of the suits began a conversation with the butcher while the other walked around the shop and stood by the door, blocking my exit. Seems like I was going to be collateral damage.

"How do you want to pay for this?" the butcher asked when he had finished filling the order. "Cash or charge?"

I noticed he kept his hand on the cleaver as the suit approached the counter. The one by the door shifted over and locked it. The one at the cashier stepped back, reached into his jacket and pulled out an enormous hand-cannon.

Looking closely, I saw it was a modified Desert Eagle .50 caliber. These vampires came prepared to take down a werewolf. The only problem was they weren't facing a werewolf. A .50 caliber silver round would stop all except the largest werewolf. If the butcher was what I thought he was, a .50 caliber round would only piss him off, silver or not.

The vampire at the door followed his lead and pulled out a similar weapon.

"That's some serious hardware," I said. "You sure

you need all that firepower for one butcher?"

He ignored me and focused on the butcher. For a brief moment, I thought about the Grim Whisper, and a tinge of barrel-envy hit me. It's not the size of the barrel, but the stopping power that matters, I told myself.

"How about silver?" the vampire at the cashier said.

"You must have me confused with someone else," the butcher said with one hand up. The other rested lightly on the cleaver next to him. "I don't want any trouble. Just take the money."

"We're not here for money. We know what you are, dog."

The vampire at the cashier took a step forward to threaten the butcher with the gun, pushing it forward. It was a mistake.

In the space of half a second, the cleaver flew up from the counter, sliced through the air and the vampire's wrist in one motion. It liberated the hand holding the gun from its body as it sailed to the side. The butcher leaped over the counter in an incredible display of grace and power and landed on the screaming vampire's chest, driving him into the floor. A heavy-booted kick knocked him out a second later.

The vampire at the door took aim as I grabbed his arm from the side and locked the elbow while stripping the oversized gun from his hand. The butcher appeared a second later with a fist to the vampire's head that sent him across the shop floor. He was unconscious by the time he slid next to his partner.

I stood there with a large gun and a larger butcher looking down at me menacingly. I turned the gun around slowly and handed it to him butt-first. He took it and nodded.

"Thanks," he said as he ejected the magazine. He made his way to the other side of the shop, located the other gun, and did the same, making sure the chambers were empty as well.

"Dissatisfied customers?" I asked, looking down at the vampires. "Looks like some people take their meat seriously."

"You have no idea," he said and cracked a smile while he outstretched a hand. "James. Friends call me 'Jimmy the Cleaver.'"

His hand was easily twice the size of mine and I had no doubt he could pulverize the bones in my hand with a minimal show of force. I was glad he didn't feel the need to show me how strong he was.

"Simon—Simon Strong. I live a block away in the monstrosity over there," I said and pointed at the Moscow.

"The Moscow? Yeah that's one ugly building, but the landlord seems nice, for an ice queen," he said.

"Jimmy the Cleaver—I can see why," I said. "What's a Werebear doing in the city? I thought you all stayed up north, away from the densely populated areas?"

Jimmy gave me an appraising look. "Not bad. Most think we're wolves, like these two rocket scientists here," he said, briefly looking down. "I got tired of country life and came down for a change of pace. How'd you know?"

"I ran into a Werebear sleuth a few years back. The scent is, no offense, unmistakable," I said. "It was led by a Were named Dov."

He nodded. "Dov is a good leader. Met him a few times before coming down here. He warned me this could happen."

"You could tell the Council. I'm pretty sure this is an unsanctioned attack."

"Dark Council knows I'm here, but I get a visit like this at least once a month," he said. "Are you going to be okay? I liked your move back there. You may get some backlash from the Council."

"No worries, I'm already on their shit list. This isn't going to make things any worse."

He reached into a pocket and pulled out his phone. "Gimme a sec," he said. "I need to call this in."

I checked the vampires. They were still alive, but they had no ID on them. Hit teams usually ran dark. Wouldn't make much sense to have their Resolution Team member cards on them, but I had to check just in case.

"Yeah, I have two leeches here who wanted to give me a silver welcome," Jimmy said into the phone. "Have them picked up before sunrise or I leave them outside for a tan."

He hung up the phone and picked up the vampires —one in each arm—and threw them into the freezer.

"Would you really leave them outside to burn?"

"Nah, but if I don't say that they drag their feet and I'm stuck with frozen vampire for days," he said. "This way they'll pick them up tonight."

"Who picks them up?"

"A Council extraction team, from the looks of it," he said. "Very apologetic, of course."

"I have an acquaintance on the Council. I could ask

her to make your shop neutral ground, if you want."

"What does that mean 'neutral ground'?"

"If she agrees, it means your shop can be a meeting place for mediations and accords," I said, looking around. "You would have to clear out some space and put in some tables, but it would mean no more attacks on you or your shop."

"No more attacks, really?" he asked. "Just by adding tables?"

"Well, tables and agreeing to let all supernaturals meet here as a safe space."

"And I won't get any more visits from the rookie welcoming committee?"

"Trust me, if this is neutral ground and someone is going to attack, it will be major league dangerous," I said.

He smiled. "At least that I can deal with. These attacks are more annoying than anything else," he said. "They scare off my customers and I can't hire help."

I nodded. "Council takes it seriously when an attack takes place on neutral ground. It brings the hammer down—hard."

"How hard? Since they aren't stopping these attacks and I'm pretty sure someone on the Council knows about them."

"Violation of neutral territory is usually answered with execution."

"Well, shit," Jimmy said and rubbed his beard, "they sound as serious as Weres. If you could swing that, Simon, I can guarantee you the freshest cuts of meat for the rest of your life, on the house." He sniffed the air. "You aren't vegan, are you?"

I laughed and pointed to my bag from Polanco's.

"The beef is mine, but the salad is for my partner. That's some nose."

"Okay, just checking," he said. "I smelled the salad too. So how about it—free meat for life?"

"How about you owe me a favor and we call it even?" I said, extending a hand. "Deal?"

"Deal," he said, smiling as he shook my hand and threatened to dislocate my shoulder.

He sniffed the air around me. "You're human, but there is something a little off about you," he said and shook his head. "Something not quite right."

"So my friends tell me. I should be seeing my Council contact later tonight. I'll bring it up and let you know."

"I would appreciate it. It means I could hire some employees if I don't have to worry about monthly attacks."

We shook again and I left the butcher shop, heading for the Moscow, when my phone rang. I picked it up on the third ring.

"I hear you've been making some new friends."

It was Hades.

"You could say that. Any way you could put a leash on him?"

"We need to talk."

"I thought that's what we were doing?"

"Strong, one day your mouth is going to get your ass in so deep, no one will be able to save you."

Getting my ass in deep was just too easy so I opted for defiance. "Who says I need saving? We've been doing fine so far."

"Only because you don't know what you're facing. I have new information for you," he said. "Come see me when you're done. Oh, and if I were you, I would hurry home—you have visitors."

"How the hell do you know—?" Several seconds went by before I realized I was speaking to myself. Hades had hung up. I started running. I stopped on the corner and made a call. I had a feeling I knew who the visitors were.

I entered the Moscow as a deep purple 1967 Pontiac GTO cruise machine with tinted windows screeched to a stop in front of the building. I took a brief moment to appreciate the classic, lovingly referred to as the Goat, and turned back to Andrei as I pulled out my phone to call Monty.

"Has anyone come in here in the last few hours?" I asked him. "Men in suits, dark glasses, with guns?"

"Nyet, no. No men in suits."

"Thanks," I said as I headed for the stairs. I pressed Monty's speed dial on my phone and heard the ring behind me. Monty was entering the building and handing some keys to the valet.

"He called you too, I assume," he said as he caught up to me. "Since when does Hades make courtesy calls?"

"Since never," I said as we headed up the stairs. "This smells like a setup."

I opened my coat to access the Ebonsoul and gently pushed the second floor stairwell door enough to look down the hallway. Our front door was ajar and I could hear voices inside.

"Monty, Olga will kill us if we destroy her building.

Well, she'll kill you and hurt me," I whispered. "Can we do this with minimal obliteration?"

"You say that like my sole purpose is to go around inflicting property damage," he answered.

"Less property damage would be great, especially in the building where we live and do business," I said, poking my head out again. "You don't see me shooting up everything in sight, do you?"

"You're firing *bullets*," he said. "I'm casting spells and unleashing unstable forces of energy and matter."

"Exactly. I would appreciate a little more stability and precision from your end, if you don't mind. Don't they teach you control in mage school?"

"If they didn't, we wouldn't be having this conversation. Let's go."

We slid up to the front door and stood on either side. I noticed the offices of Christye, Blahq, and Doil were closed for the day, as usual. I was beginning to wonder if they did any business at all. Voices drifted out to us from inside our space.

"Get that door open or I swear I'll kill you where you stand," a voice said. "And move that mountain of filth away from me."

"Sounds like Yama is down," I whispered and slid across the wall. "What accent is that?"

"It's a brogue, Irish, which means they're after our guest," he said. "Let's try diplomacy first."

"Are you sure? That one didn't sound in a diplomatic mood."

Monty pushed open the door and I took in the scene. It was a smaller group than what we faced at the blood bank. Three vampires were working on the vault door with blowtorches. Two more stood near the kitchen, one of them looking in my fridge for I don't know what. Another two stood to the side of the door and pulled guns similar to the one I had seen in the butcher shop.

"Is there a sale on these things?" I said as I stared down the barrel of another oversized hand-cannon. "Compensating much?"

The leader I guessed was the angry-looking vampire standing behind the three working on the door. He turned to us as we entered the room. He was tall and dressed in what I started to call the "trenchy villain" look—long black trench coat, lots of black clothing underneath, accessorized with black highlights. Ken would be proud.

They all wore a similar uniform and I figured this must be their version of a hit team. No dark suits, just lots of trench coats. Each of the coats had a red emblem I recognized on the right shoulder. It was a Claddagh with a sword running through the center of the heart.

"How can we help you?" Monty asked and unbuttoned his jacket.

I didn't see any orbs of energy in Monty's hands, which meant he was really going to try to talk them down.

"You could start by opening this door," Angry Leader said, pointing at the darkroom.

"I'm afraid we can't do that," Monty answered, slowly shaking his head. "The young woman in that room is under our care."

"That bitch is shunned!" the leader yelled. "Now

either you open the door or we force you to open it."

"She is currently being protected by the Dark Council," Monty said. "If you violate that protection —"

"Does it look like I give a flying shite about your Dark Council? *Teigh transa ort fein*," he said and spit on the floor.

"I'm going to guess that's not Irish for 'let's be friends,'" I said. "Is it?"

Monty shook his head again and flexed his jaw. Never a good sign.

"Open the door," the leader said, "before I drain you both."

"We can't," I said, holding my hands up. "It locks from the inside and I don't think she wants to come out and say hello to—who are you guys, anyway? The Unfriendlies?"

"Then what use are you?" he said. "Kill them."

"Well, that's just rude," I said and ducked as I pulled out the Ebonsoul.

I stabbed the vampire to my left in the leg and rolled next to him as the one on my right fired at me and missed. Monty advanced on the leader. I shot the vampire next to me with Grim Whisper, and he crumbled into a pile of dust. *So glad I remembered to pack the runed bullets.*

This mobilized the rest of the room.

"Monty," I said, as a bullet punched through my shoulder and spun me around into the fist of the vampire who had missed earlier. My head rocked back from the blow and stars filled the edges of my vision as I staggered back. He buried a kick in my stomach and sent me across the room. "Shit, don't kill them all," I managed to get out as I landed hard on my back.

The air rushed out of my lungs as the vampire leaped at me. I pressed the orb on the mala and he froze several feet above me for half a second with a surprised look on his face. The shield reversed his direction and slammed him into the ceiling. He landed in a dazed heap. I walked over to where he lay and put a bullet into him. He went from vampire to dust in less than a second. My shoulder was screaming at me as I felt it heal.

"Monty, keep the leader alive," I said as I caught my breath. "We need information."

"No," Monty said, and I didn't like the tone of his voice. "They have entered our home and should suffer. They deserve to die."

"Whoa, Monty? Deserve to die? What happened to diplomacy?" I said quickly as I holstered Grim Whisper.

"I've realized that it doesn't work."

"That lasted all of ten seconds. How about we dial it back a bit?"

Black rotating discs of energy formed in his hands as he advanced. The whirring sound they made transported me instantly to a dentist's chair. It set my teeth on edge and raised the hairs on the back of my neck.

"Stay back, Simon," he said, his voice full of menace.

"Monty, what the hell is that? That is definitely not dialing it back."

He let the discs go. They hummed through the air— two buzz saws of death. The vampires near the kitchen never had a chance. The discs sliced through them effortlessly before cutting holes through the wall and disappearing.

Their upper bodies fell away from their legs. Screams of agony filled the room as their torsos flailed briefly on the floor before growing still.

"Bloody hell, Monty," I whispered. "What're you doing?"

"I'm neutralizing the threat. I'm tired of playing nice, of observing rules of warfare. No more."

"This isn't you, Monty," I said, slowly raising my empty hand. "Don't do this. Not like this."

"You don't know me; this is what I do best."

He turned to face me and I saw his irises. They were solid black with a glowing ring of gold. In that moment, I realized three things: Monty was still seriously pissed about Roxanne—so much for venting, the vampires in the room were all dead—they just didn't know it yet, and he was scarier than anything we had ever faced.

The three vampires at the vault door dropped the blowtorches and bolted. Monty sent a disc after them without taking his eyes off the leader. I sliced through it with the Ebonsoul and it exploded with a thump, launching me over the sofa as I landed with a thud.

"Monty, stop." I groaned as I stood shakily.

"No, Simon. I told you to stay back. Don't get in my way again."

His voice had gone down a few octaves and I considered running for the door myself, but he was my friend, not a cold-blooded murderer. He would never forgive himself if I let him continue this way.

I did the only thing I could do.

NINETEEN

STOPPING TIME IS a lot trickier than it sounds. According to Monty, I wasn't actually stopping time but stepping outside of it. I wasn't a quantum physicist, or any other kind of physicist for that matter, so he explained it as simply as possible. Time is similar to a river and when I activated my mark, I stepped out of the river for a short amount of time while it continued to flow.

I couldn't go back or forward along the river. I had to step back in wherever I stepped out. At that point in the explanation, I began getting a headache.

Bottom line was I could stop time for ten seconds. When the ten seconds was up, I would be in the same location chronologically before I activated the mark. Anything I altered would take effect after the ten seconds were up.

In this case, what I wanted was Karma to show up. I needed her to stop Monty from bisecting this vampire and I didn't think ten seconds was going to be enough time to act.

I placed my right hand on my left, making sure to touch the two points of the endless knot with my thumb and index fingers, and focused. White light raced from each end and connected at the center and the world around me took on a hazy feel. Everything fell out of focus as I looked around.

The smell of lotus flowers filled the room and I smiled. Karma materialized in front of me. She was doing the college student look again—blue jeans, comfortable boots, and a black sweater. She wore a black baseball cap that read BITCH in bold red letters, and the smile across her lips looked dangerous. The little voice that warned me of imminent threats began wailing. This may have been a mistake.

"Did you just try and *summon* me?" she said coyly and stepped close. The lotus smell wrapped itself around me, making it hard to breathe.

"I need your help," I whispered. "It's Monty."

I pointed behind her but she ignored my gesture. The backhand rocked my jaw, lifted me off my feet, and planted me on the floor in front of her. The room swam for a few seconds as I got my bearings. After the earlier vampire treatment, a concussion wasn't out of the question.

She crouched down so that we were face-to-face when she spoke. The feral look in her eyes made me instantly regret calling her.

"I'm not your *genie*, that you think you can call when it all goes to shit. Do you know who I am?"

At this point, I wasn't sure who *I* was, but I didn't say that since she was being so giving with head shots.

"Karma?" I hazarded a guess. "*The* Karma?"

"Exactly. Now listen closely, Simon," she said and cupped my chin and stood, bringing me effortlessly to my feet. "I don't care if Monty wants to dust this vampire."

"But you're—?"

"I'm the aftermath. I reap what you sow. I'm the effect to your cause," she said. "I don't do interventions—I do reckonings."

"I thought—" I started.

"You thought wrong and I've interfered enough," she replied and her voice softened. "I like you, Simon, I do. You even wear my mark, but I can't have favorites."

"I'm not asking to be your favorite," I said. "I just need you to—"

"Don't try and summon me again," she said, her voice hard. "If I could I would remove your mark—don't make me remove your arm."

"I won't," I said, my mind racing. Monty was going to kill this vampire in a fit of rage and I couldn't stop him. "My arm?"

"You'd better hurry and help your friend. Your twenty seconds will start the moment I'm gone."

She gave me a quick wink, smiled, and disappeared.

Twenty seconds?

I had to act fast. It was ten seconds more than I usually had. I didn't know how she did it, I only cared that she had given me more time.

I pulled out the silver restraints we used for werewolf takedowns. If I put them on Monty, he would blast right through them and the vampire. Silver didn't slow him down much. I'd seen him take a silver round and not even blink as he responded with a fireball.

My only option was the vampire. The restraints weren't designed for them, but it was the best idea I had. I ran over to the leader of the Unfriendlies and attached them to his wrists. They gave off a brief orange glow as they locked closed.

I moved back to Monty, moved him out of our office, and locked the door on him. The four-inch slab of steel was only slightly weaker than the vault door to the darkroom. It made me wonder how they got in in the first place.

We really need better security.

Monty had runed it himself and I requested he make it everything-proof. I gave it about a minute—two, tops before he shredded it. I really hoped those restraints would slow the vampire down. I had just locked myself in a room with an angry vampire, and the one person with the power to take it down was locked outside. I pulled out Grim Whisper and took aim.

Everything snapped back into focus and time flowed.

"Bloody hell! Simon!" Monty yelled from outside. "Open the door!"

He pounded on the door hard enough for me to be concerned it would crumple under his assault.

"I'm not opening it until you calm down, Monty," I yelled back. "Do some breathing exercises or whatever it is mages do."

"I'm calm, now open the door," he said.

I could hear the tension in his voice as he spoke through gritted teeth.

"Liar. Go take a walk around the block. I got this."

The leader of the Unfriendlies looked at me and grinned.

"You've grown tired of life, boy?" he said. "You're no match for me, even with your magical bullets."

Since he wasn't writhing on the floor in agony, I figured the restraints weren't working, until I smelled burning flesh. Smoke was rising from his wrists. The vampire began clawing at the restraints, ripping his own flesh in the process.

"Won't work," I said and kept Grim Whisper pointed at him. "You can't take them off."

"I'll kill you!" he screamed as he kept at the restraints. "I'll drain you dry and then make you beg for death."

"Or you can leave Georgianna alone and leave here in one piece," I said calmly. "Your call."

"We never reverse a shunning. She's not one of us and needs to be removed."

"You mean killed because she's different?"

"She's an abomination to our house. She needs to be purged."

"Excuse me?" I asked. "Are you really standing there telling me—I can't believe you. I should just shoot you and get it over with."

Monty had gone silent, which worried me, but I didn't dare take my eyes off the vampire. Behind the leader of the Unfriendlies, a figure materialized. It was Michiko. I lowered Grim Whisper, and the vampire thought I was giving up—mistake. He took two steps forward and jerked back as Michiko whiplashed him to the floor with enough force to crack the parquet.

She grabbed him by the neck and held him aloft. He gasped with pain at the suddenness of being whisked off his feet. She narrowed her eyes at me and drew her lips tight with a sharp intake of breath. Her hand began smoking where she held him.

"Simon, please remove the restraints. They're distracting,"

I kept Grim Whisper pointed at him as I walked over. I placed my hand on each of the restraints and they clicked open. Monty had keyed them to our touch. I took them off the vampire and stepped back just as Monty crashed through the living room window.

"You could have just knocked," I said, and he stared daggers at me. I walked over to the broken window. "Olga is going to have a fit if she sees this."

He dusted off the glass and walked over to where Michiko stood. He gave her a brief nod, which she returned. The darkroom door opened and Georgianna poked her head out.

"What is your name?" Michiko asked the vamp. "Lying will only end your life. I advise against it."

"That's Colin," Georgianna said. "He's one of the elders of our clan."

"Bitch, I'm going to kill you. I'm—" he said before Michiko cut his words short by applying pressure to his neck.

"He invaded our home and attacked us," Monty said. "I claim the right of retaliation."

"No," Michiko said. "I can't grant you that. This shunning is more complicated than it seems. If you kill him, it will escalate matters and force my hand. As it stands, we can no longer relocate her."

Monty stood perfectly still for a few moments. I stole a glance at his eyes for gold circles to make sure he didn't go executioner on us but they remained normal. After a few more seconds, he gave a sharp nod.

I let out a breath.

"Then you will provide reparations for the damage incurred," he said. "And restore the offices to their previous state."

"Of course," Michiko answered and nodded. "Everything will be covered by the Dark Council. Anything else?"

"Since you can't relocate her, we will take her as our charge," he said, gesturing to Georgianna. "Until other options can be explored."

"You overstep your bounds, mage," Michiko said, her voice tight. "She isn't a mage, she's a vampire."

"Who's been shunned by her own kind," Monty said and looked around. "Where is your usual escort? You aren't even here officially, are you?"

Michiko smiled. I'd seen her give that same smile to future victims. "Well played, mage."

"Are you sure it's a good idea to piss off the very powerful vampire in the room?" I whispered to him.

"Are we in agreement?" Monty asked, ignoring me.

"I will return this filth to his clan and you will keep her safe as your charge," Michiko said, glancing at Colin. "As you may have guessed, she has special needs."

"It would explain the shunning," Monty answered. "We will address her needs."

"It would be great if you could explain it to me

while you're at it," I said, confused.

Michiko stepped close to me, still holding Colin like a ragdoll.

"You are fortunate to have your mage friend, Simon-kun."

"I don't know if I'd use the word fortunate. It's probably closer to cursed," I said, looking down into her eyes. "I need a favor."

"What kind of favor?" she asked with a dangerous smile. "Is this something better discussed in private?"

"No, no, not that kind of favor," I said and took a step back. "I need a location made neutral territory."

"This is no easy task. Where?"

"The Randy Rump—the butcher a block away from here," I said. "We don't have neutral territory downtown."

"The butcher shop owned by the Werebear?" she asked.

"You know it?" I asked, surprised.

She gave me the 'sometimes I wonder how your brain even operates' look and nodded. "Yes, I know it, but it's not my decision alone. I will bring it before the Council."

"Thanks, I really appreciate it," I said, and she stepped close again.

She gave me one of her rare smiles and then grew serious.

"Your security is pathetic; get it fixed. A work crew will be here within the hour to repair the damage."

"What about your mountain?" I asked, looking at the prone form of Yama. "He wasn't much of a deterrent now."

"Let him regain his honor, or end his life," she replied dismissively. "I will leave that up to you. I have no use for him."

She could be one cold-hearted bitch. Not that I would ever say that to her face. I nodded and shuddered as she ran her finger across my cheek.

"I will see you again soon," she said, and nicked my cheek, drawing blood. "Try to stay alive until then."

"Top of my to-do list."

She stepped back and vanished, taking Colin the Unfriendly with her. I turned to assess the damage, which was extensive.

"Well, she's right about our security, or lack thereof," Monty grumbled as he made his way around the debris of his entrance. "Especially when she comes and goes as she pleases."

"Monty, what the hell just happened?"

TWENTY

MONTY BUZZED DOWNSTAIRS and handed me the spare set of keys to the Goat. The Pontiac GTO got its name from the Ferrari 250 GTO, a rare and beautiful piece of automotive art. The GTO stands for Grand Tourismo Omologato. I'm sure no one wanted to say that mouthful—so GTO became Goat, and a legendary muscle car was christened.

"I'm not driving that monstrosity," he said. "It was all I could do to get here in one piece. Bloody steering wheel is on the wrong side."

"I don't think you will be attacked again," I said to Georgianna. "Try and get Yama the Mountain Range conscious and we'll talk when we get back."

"I'll clean up some of this mess in the meantime," she said. "Tristan, thank you. I really appreciate what you did for me."

"Don't make me regret it," Monty said and headed out the door. "Every action you take from now on reflects on us."

"Make sure this door is locked," I said, pulling the door behind me. "Michiko's people will probably just show up. Don't attack them: we need the repairs done."

"Got it and thank you too, Simon," she said as she approached the door. "I don't know how you stood up to a vampire alone."

"As long as I have my friends, I'm never alone," I said, and headed out the door to catch up with Monty.

Andrei stood in the lobby by the entrance of the building. I was surprised Olga wasn't there to greet me in all her frigid glory considering the amount of noise we made. He gave me a knowing nod and I knew he had avoided calling her.

"Sorry about all the noise," I said.

"You fix by tomorrow," he said. It wasn't a question.

I held out my hand and we shook.

"Thank you. I owe you."

"Da, go, talk to scary friend. Fix his face. He looks angry," he said, and gestured with his chin at Monty.

"I'll do that," I said and stepped outside into the evening cold where Monty was waiting.

We stood in front of the building in silence. The valet pulled the Purple Goat up to the entrance. It rumbled to a stop as I admired the classic lines. He handed the keys to Monty and headed inside.

"Monty—" I started.

"You used the mark. Did you summon her?"

"Yes, you didn't give me an option, Monty. You went full Vader on me," I said, looking out into the cold night. "I don't know how I summoned her, but I did."

"I apologize, Simon," he said after a pause. "It's not like me to lose control like that."

"You *never* lose control. What happened?"

"The situation brought up bad memories. It was a little too close to home," he said. "It won't happen again, you have my word."

"If I get lost in the Ebonsoul and you go terminator like that, it would be—"

"The outcome would be horrific," he whispered. "I'll make sure that doesn't come to pass."

"I know you're worried about Roxanne—"

"Don't," he said, raising a hand and cutting me off. "If you try and make a bloody funny remark, I'll test your immortality myself."

"I was just going to say I know you're concerned," I said.

"You've no idea and we're wasting time. Let's go."

I lifted my hands in surrender as he walked over to the passenger side and got in. He was never one for overt displays of emotion and he was right. As close as we were, I didn't know much about him or his past. I only knew I trusted him with my life. Right now that would have to be enough.

I got in the Goat and fastened my seatbelt. The engine roared and settled into a purr and I felt the vibration in my gut. I pulled off and jumped on the West Side Highway headed downtown to Water Street and Hades.

"You couldn't get it in a different color? I mean, purple?"

"The actual color is Byzantium, not purple, and apparently the color serves a purpose, according to Cecil," he said.

"Right, it was probably a color he just wanted to

offload and lucky us, we get the Purple Goat," I muttered under my breath.

Monty sighed and looked out the window.

"Did Hades say what he wanted? He was terse when we spoke," he said.

"Just that he had information we needed and we're in over our heads. Facing exploding sorcerers, Chaos, and the ogre made that kind of obvious, though."

"He knows Chaos is involved? Has Ramirez called us with that inventory from the museum?"

"Not yet," I said and pulled out my phone.

"Sorry, what are you doing?" Monty asked with alarm.

"I'm calling Ramirez," I said while swerving around traffic. "What does it look like I'm doing?"

"Getting us killed," he said and snatched my phone. "Focus on the driving, please."

Monty pressed the speed dial I had for Ramirez. It rang several times before he picked up.

"Put it on speaker," I said. "Ramirez, any news?"

"Oh, you want news?" he snapped back. "I have the museum director on my ass because their entire façade is *missing*. I have my boss on my ass for the damage to the museum and the squad cars."

"NYTF brass loves to complain, you know that. They only see numbers."

"I know," he said and sighed. "Several of my guys are still going through psych eval because they saw something but don't know *what* they saw."

"I could explain—" I offered.

"Don't bother. You'll only make things worse. On top of that the media is here making it a PR nightmare clusterfuck. Any other *news* you would like?"

"I was really thinking more about the museum inventory, but the rest of that sounds like you have your hands full. Do you want me to call you back?"

"I don't want you to call me at all," he said. "You think you could swing that?"

"Ramirez," Monty said, "I think the inventory is crucial to finding out why they were under attack."

"So far, all I know is the museum was showing an exhibit on the supernatural war called 'War & Peace.' They had drawings and artifacts from the war on display."

"Can you check to see if any of the artifacts are missing?" Monty asked and rubbed his chin. "Also who organized the exhibit?"

"Right now they're still dealing with the fact that most of the front of the museum is missing. As soon as I get the list and the organizer, I'll call you."

He hung up and Monty looked off into the distance. I could tell he was trying to make sense of something.

"How many artifacts from the war survived?" I asked.

"Quite a few, but they were mostly innocuous items, like old uniforms and things of that nature. The dangerous items were removed to different vaults throughout the world."

"Who oversaw the removal of those?"

"Each respective government had a representative present," he said. "The magical items were handled by the Mage Consortium Reclamation Unit."

"The what?"

"The mage schools were not enough individually, so

a group was formed during the war comprised of the best of each school," he said. "I was part of the MBU —the battle unit. After the war, another group was created—MCRU— and their job was to scour the battlefields for anything magical that was potentially dangerous and to secure it."

I parked the Goat in front of One New York Plaza and got out. I checked the keys for a fob to lock the car and saw none.

"How do we lock the car? Key, or do I wave my hands over it in special magical sequence?"

"Don't be ridiculous. Put your thumb on the handle," Monty answered, pointing at the door. "Then step back."

I did as he instructed and heard a metal clang as the doors locked. Something that sounded like a hammer striking an anvil came from under the hood. An orange glow flashed over the Goat and faded slowly.

"It's locked now," he said, stepping away from the car. "The engine is inoperable until we unlock it."

"What was the glow? Force field?" I asked, gently touching the Goat. Nothing happened.

"No, it's a runic defense to prevent a magical attack or tampering."

"Oh, a *magical* force field. Nice."

"Runic defense—not a force field of any kind."

"Biometric scanner? That impressive," I said, looking at the now locked car. "How did he get my fingerprint?"

"Cecil is very thorough." Monty approached the entrance, looking at the top floors. "Hades keeps odd hours."

"He probably doesn't sleep, being a god and all."

"It's possible, but he could've told us whatever it was when we were here yesterday," Monty said.

"You think it's possible the MCRU missed something and it ended up in the museum? Or someone kept an artifact?"

"I suppose it's possible," Monty answered. "It was right after the war. Things were disorganized for several days."

We entered the lobby. The security men next to the massive wooden reception desk looked up and motioned for us to approach. We placed our credentials on the desk. It was a different receptionist, though she had a similar appearance—tall, sky-blue eyes, and almost white blond hair.

"Is she a—?" I started.

"Yes, she is," Monty said, looking at the receptionist. "I believe he's expecting us."

"He is," she said. "Someone will be down shortly to escort you. Please have a seat."

She returned our credentials and gestured to the waiting area. A steaming kettle was on a tray with cups next to it. Monty fixed himself a cup and sighed as he sat down to drink it.

"Isn't it a little late for tea?"

"No such thing," he said and sipped.

"He takes his security seriously," I said as I sat in one of the chairs opposite Monty. "Maybe we should increase the runes around the office?"

"Yes, because they are so effective against your vampire coming and going as she pleases," he said. "We need a deterrent *inside* the office. If I rune the interior, the chances of it being triggered by you or one of our new guests makes it too dangerous."

"When you spoke to Hades, did he say anything about 'visitors in the office'?"

Monty nodded. "That was the only reason I drove back in that beast of a car," he said.

"How did he know we had visitors in the office?"

"We can ask him, though I doubt he will answer," Monty said, looking up as he put his cup down.

The same blonde from the day before walked over to us. This time she wore a black business suit with matching heels. It had the same sheen as her other suit.

"Good evening," she said. "This way, please."

We entered the elevator and the doors whispered closed behind us. She inserted a key next to the button for the penthouse and pressed a button labeled PH.

"I have another question for you. Do you mind?" I said.

"Ask," she said.

I saw Monty look at me and shake his head. He stepped back and to the side, probably to give the Valkyrie enough room to swing at me.

"Your suit. What is it made of? That's unlike any fabric I've ever seen."

"It's not fabric. Its drakescale," she said.

"You mean dragon scale? As in a real dragon?"

"Think chainmail, only one hundred times stronger," she said as the doors opened to our floor. "Besides, we both know 'real dragons' don't exist."

Monty and I stepped out as she remained inside the elevator.

"Neither do Valkyries, and yet here you are," I said.

"Who's your tailor?"

"Good evening, gentlemen," she said with a smile as the doors closed.

"'Who's your tailor?' Really?" Monty said. "Why didn't you ask her out for coffee and biscuits?"

"Do you think she would've accepted? Could you imagine the stories she could tell?"

"I can imagine what your vampire would do," he said as we approached Hades's office. "Do you recall the last 'date' you were on?"

I shuddered at the memory. Everything had gone well until Michiko showed up and expressed her disapproval—violently.

"Never mind," I said. "Okay, how do you want to play this?"

"We go in, see what he wants and we leave with our lives," Monty answered as he adjusted his jacket. "That is the general plan."

"Good plan," I said and pushed open the door.

Across the sea of Persian rug sat Hades behind his redwood of a desk. Behind him and to his right stood Corbel as stoic as a Queen's Guard. Hades was dressed in a beige suit, cream shirt, and a burnt sienna tie. He looked impeccable enough to make Piero drool with admiration. A few steps in, I noticed the smell.

"Monty, did you eat eggs this morning?"

"Shut it, now," he said under his breath. "It's brimstone, or what you know as sulfur."

"It's an assault on my nose is what it is. Damn," I said in between gasps. "Hades, what's with the smell? Did something die in here?"

"Your humor never ceases to amuse, Simon," Hades

said with a tight smile. "Please, sit down, the both of you."

We approached the desk and sat in his fancy English chairs. I tried my best to hold my breath and failed. I saw several pictures laid out on top of his desk. He picked up one and passed it to Corbel.

"How is the investigation proceeding?" Hades asked. "Have you located the Ferryman?"

"Not yet," Monty said. "It would appear Chaos is involved somehow."

Corbel came over to our side of the massive desk and the smell intensified.

"Whoa," I said, gasping. "You need to change that cologne. What is that, Essence of Death?"

"Actually, yes," Hades said with a smile. "Corbel has been picking up a package for the both of you."

"If it smells like that, I politely decline said package, thank you, but no thanks," I said.

"First things first," Hades said. Corbel handed Monty the photo.

"Do you recognize that drawing?" Hades steepled his fingers as he reclined in his chair.

Monty looked at the photo and the color slowly drained from his face. He looked up and Hades nodded at him.

"This can't be—?" Monty started.

"Real?" Hades asked. "It's real."

"Impossible," Monty whispered, putting the photo down on the desk. "Where did you get this?"

"Improbable, but not impossible," Hades said and held out another picture for Corbel, who walked over and spread more of his nose-battering aroma. My eyes were beginning to tear up at this point.

"They were destroyed, all of them," Monty said. "Where was this taken?"

"That was on display at MoMA. Which, as I understand, has suffered some vandalism?"

"Something like that," I said as Monty slid the picture to me. It showed a framed canvas with what appeared to be a large rune drawn in blood. "What's this?"

"Tristan?" Hades said. "Would you like to illuminate him?"

"That is the null rune," he said like I understood what he meant.

"Like the rune of negation Ramirez has?" I said, looking at the picture. "Is this one of those weapons the mages created during the war?"

When I didn't get a response, I looked up and saw Monty holding another picture. He was visibly shaken and put the picture back on the desk. I picked it up and saw a small pedestal holding what could only be described as an amulet.

"How could they miss that?" Monty asked himself. "Of all things, they missed that?"

"Indeed," Hades said. "It would seem there was some corruption amongst the mages to overlook an artifact this powerful."

My nose sighed in relief as Corbel went back to his post, taking the odor of destruction away from us.

"Wait a minute," I said, pointing at the second picture. "I've seen this."

"I know what he wants," Monty said and turned to me. "Wait, what did you say?"

"I've seen this pendant before. Chaos was wearing it when he entered the stasis."

Hades stood and walked to the window behind his desk.

"Do you understand now, Tristan?" Hades said.

"Back up," I said, holding the picture. "What is this thing?"

"That is an Infinite Amulet," Monty said. "It's made to contain and weaponize the null rune."

"This null rune is worse than the negation rune?"

"By several magnitudes of order," Hades answered and placed a palm against the window. "But Chaos can't activate the rune or the pendant."

"Why not?" I asked. "It looks like he has everything he needs."

Not yet," Hades said. "He needs a sacrifice, given freely and willingly."

"What kind of sacrifice?" I asked.

"He needs the essence of sorcerers and the blood of a very special mage to activate the rune and then merge it with the amulet. Isn't that right, Tristan?"

"Ten sorcerers and one Golden Circle mage are required to activate the amulet," Monty said. "The essence of the sorcerers is absorbed by the mage who then wields the amulet. It's the ultimate weapon. Nothing can stand against it."

That's when it hit me.

"Roxanne," I whispered. "He doesn't want her. He wants you."

TWENTY-ONE

"YOU SHOULD BE getting a summons from him soon," Hades said as he sat at his desk. "He will try to force your hand. Your best option is to let her die."

"Unacceptable," Monty said as his jaw flexed. "That option is not on the table."

"What does he want? Why go through all of this?" I said.

"Chaos is actually very simple in his motivation," Hades answered. "He always has been. He wants the end."

"The end of what?" I asked.

"Of everything," Hades said, waving a hand. "Especially humanity."

"Why not just wage war? He's a god, after all. Just like the rest of you."

"No, not like us. He's one of the Old Ones. No longer actively worshipped," Hades said. "We could stop him if he rose to wage war against us."

"Then why not go stop him now?" I said. "That

sounds like an excellent plan."

"Unless directly threatened, the others will not act. We prefer the status quo," Hades said. "With the amulet, however, he would be too powerful. He could start another supernatural war that would involve the gods themselves."

"He *has* the amulet, so how are we supposed to stop him?" I said.

"True, but it's not active," Hades replied. "At this moment it's just jewelry. Find a way to get it back."

"Just us two? Can't you lend us, like, an undead army or some of the Valkyries?"

"No, if I'm seen to favor you with my participation, it could set off an unpredictable chain of events," Hades said. "Even I have enemies. If Charon is still missing, it means he still needs sorcerers."

"So we need to find Charon and steal back the amulet before he somehow forces Monty to give up his blood and merge the rune and destroys us all."

"Seems like you have a handle on it, yes," Hades said. "I have every confidence in your abilities."

"This is suicide," I said angrily as I stood. "I'm so tired of you gods playing your games and not getting your hands dirty."

"Measure your words, Strong," Hades warned as he stood. "They may be your last."

"Simon," Monty warned, "it may be time for us to leave."

"No, Monty," I said. "What's he going to do, kill me? Kali already took care of that. Besides, who's going to go on his suicide run if he kills us?"

"There are many things worse than death," Hades

said, every word full of menace. "You were chosen for this because you can act without serious repercussions."

"Translation—we're expendable," I said, throwing the picture I held on the desk. "Monty, yes, let's get the hell out of here."

"Sit down," Hades said. "Now."

The last word reverberated throughout his office and I actually felt the building shake. I remained on my feet and stared him down. My bowels were turning to jelly and my heart felt like I had just run two back-to-back marathons. I wanted to crawl under the desk and hide, but my brain was too stubborn to back down.

I sensed the energy around Monty and felt the heat of his orbs as he stood next to me. Corbel adjusted his position and assumed a defensive stance. Behind us, I heard the door open and several sets of footsteps enter the room.

"Well, if we're going to die, you certainly picked the best place for it," Monty whispered. "This is guaranteed to be a short trip."

"Enough," Hades whispered and gestured. It was a sort of half-wave flick of his wrist that seemed to suck the oxygen out of the room.

A shockwave raced across the floor with Hades at its epicenter. The orbs in Monty's hands vanished. Industrial-sized runes flared to life on the walls, floor, and ceiling.

Monty sat down in the chair hard, his face pale. I turned to Hades and drew the Ebonsoul. He remained motionless as Corbel advanced. Hades raised his hand and Corbel stopped moving.

"Siphoning runes," Monty whispered, trying to catch his breath. "Bollocks."

"What did you do to him?" I said and took a step forward. Corbel raised an eyebrow and I heard the metallic chorus of swords being unsheathed sing behind me.

"Nothing," Hades answered. "He'll be fine in a few minutes. Corbel, please bring their package. Ladies, I will not have need of your services, thank you."

I turned to see five Valkyrie sheath their swords and leave the room in silence, each of them fixing me with a stare designed to strike fear as they exited. It only made me angry.

I held the Ebonsoul and squeezed the hilt until my knuckles were white. Hades looked at me for a moment longer and then sat down.

"As much as I would enjoy a sparring session with you, Strong, even with your 'special situation,' it would be—pardon the pun—short-lived," he said. "Your power is not where it needs to be to face me—yet. But both of you were willing to try—what did you call it— a suicide run?"

"Shit, you set me up," I said, sheathing the Ebonsoul.

"I did no such thing," Hades said. "I merely facilitated a context to demonstrate that, despite your fear, you were the best pair for the job at hand."

He was right. The rational part of my brain knew he was right. Fighting him would be suicide, but it didn't stop us from considering it. He had proven his point. If we were insane enough to try to take him on, we were the ones to face Chaos. I sat down hard, hating that he was right.

"Bollocks," Monty whispered. "Facing Chaos and defeating him are different things."

"I'm not suggesting you defeat him," Hades answered. "Get the amulet away from him or the rune. If you can manage both, even better. Preferably without spilling any of your blood, Tristan."

"Easier said than done," I muttered, angry with myself for letting him push my buttons. "It's not like he's just going to hand them over."

"Convince him," Hades said and the smell of sulfur strangled me again. Corbel had entered the room with a large crate. "Place it over here and leave us."

Corbel placed the crate next to me.

"Thank you for sharing," I said, covering my face. "I may never smell again."

"I live for the simple pleasures," he whispered with a smile. "Draw your weapon on him again and I'll kill everything and everyone in your life."

"Next time you want to threaten me, don't use words," I replied and pulled back my coat, revealing the Ebonsoul and the Grim Whisper. "Unless this stench is your weapon, in which case I surrender—you win."

Hades coughed and Corbel bowed. He walked to the door, bowed again and left.

"Simon, you just don't know when to quit," Monty said. Most of the color had returned to his face. "He's dangerous. There's a reason they call him the 'Hound of Hades.'"

"I'm guessing it has something to do with his pungency—the man is ripe."

"Strong, honestly, I don't know how you're still

among the living," Hades said. "You're either very brave or very stupid."

"The latter," Monty said without hesitation.

"You need to get him on some kind of hygiene plan," I said, taking a deep breath. "I won't be able to smell anything for months."

"You would do well to take his threat seriously," Hades said. "He's a fearsome enemy."

"So am I. He so much as looks at me sideways or steps in my direction again, I shoot first and won't bother with questions."

Hades nodded. "Duly noted. That is for you," he said, pointing at the crate. "I hear you have been having security issues at your place of residence."

"And this is…?" I asked, wary. When a god wants to give you something, always read the fine print. Hades was known for being downright shady in negotiations and his gifts always came with strings attached.

"We're flattered, but we can't accept it—whatever it is," Monty said. "Thank you, but no."

"Every ten years, Cerberus sires offspring," Hades said, ignoring Monty.

"Wait, Cerberus, as in the three-headed dog?"

"That's called embellishment. *I* spread that rumor, Strong. Are you serious? Have you ever met a three-headed dog?" Hades asked. "Next you'll tell me you still believe in dragons?"

"We recently fought an ogre, a real ogre," I said, feeling defensive. "Are you telling me I imagined that too?"

"Well, that's different," Hades said with a smile. "Those are *real*. I will concede that you are new to all of this, Strong. I suggest you get up to speed as soon as possible. What you don't know can kill those around you."

"I take it this is his offspring?" Monty asked and looked into the crate. I followed Monty's lead and looked in too. A pair of yellow eyes stared back at me, followed by a low growl that rattled the crate.

"That is Peaches," Hades said with a small amount of pride evident in his voice.

"Not Mr. Peaches or Sir Peaches?" I said as I peered into the crate. The eyes shifted from yellow to deep red followed by a low growl.

Monty coughed and I chuckled nervously until I looked up.

"It's just Peaches," he said, glaring at me.

"Peaches? Are you serious?" I said and saw the look on Hades's face. "I mean, a seriously good name, Peaches."

"Named him myself," he said. "If I don't give him away, he'll have to be put down."

"Let him live with his dad. That way you get twice the security. Not that I can imagine anyone trying to break into Hades."

"I can tell you've never met Cerberus. He's insanely territorial and would destroy him."

"We don't have the room," Monty said, quickly looking at my face and shaking his head.

"Maybe just for a little while until you find him a new home?" I said, looking at the yellow eyes that flared red for a split second. "He can't be that bad. What breed is he?"

"There is no name for the breed he is," Hades

answered. "Cerberus was created to be the only one of his kind. The closest approximation would be a Cane Corso, but that's only in appearance."

"This means it will be massive," Monty said, shaking his head. "Cane Corso are Italian mastiffs."

"Well, I hear you have a vampire problem," Hades said. "Massive is good."

"It's not a problem, per se," I answered, glancing at Monty. "They just like to visit every so often."

"Wait, this creature—" Monty started.

"Peaches," Hades said, correcting him.

"Yes, sorry. This *Peaches* can stop the vampires from coming in unannounced?" Monty asked.

"Peaches will stop *anyone* from coming in unannounced," Hades said with a smile. "Look closer, Tristan."

Monty looked inside the crate and I saw one eyebrow go up in surprise. "Are those what I think they are?" he said.

Hades nodded. "Gets them from Cerberus. As he matures, he'll be able to communicate with his bondmate—provided they possess enough power to hear him. However, he can understand everything you say."

Monty rubbed his chin in thought. "Fine, Simon will be responsible for him."

"What? When did I agree to this?"

"It makes perfect sense," Monty said. "The vampires don't come to see me, they come to see you. One in particular especially."

"Wait, he doesn't eat humans or anything like that does he?"

Hades gave me another look. "He's a dog, Strong—have you encountered the species? He eats dog food. Oh, one last thing, one of you has to bond with him."

"Excuse me? Bond with him?" I said. "What do you mean bond with him?"

"Yes, one of you has to stick your hand in the crate and bond with him. There must be an energy transfer. What did you think I meant by *bondmate*?"

Monty crossed his arms and looked at me defiantly. "I've grown fond of my hands, thank you very much. You want him—you bond."

"Has he been fed?" I asked. "I mean recently?"

"A moment ago you were willing to fight me to your repeated death. Now you're telling me you're scared of a little dog?"

"Little dog?" I said, looking in the crate again. "I don't see anything *little* about him."

"What's the worst that can happen? You die?" Hades asked with a smile.

"When you put it like that," I said and stuck my hand in the crate.

TWENTY-TWO

"I CAN'T BELIEVE you, Monty," I said as we drove uptown. "You couldn't just add more runes to the office?"

"Your vampire seems to find a way around the rune defenses. No matter how many times I change them."

"Maybe stronger runes that could contain any unwanted visitor," I said. "You can do that."

"I've used my strongest and they don't work because of your connection to her," he replied. "Besides, now I won't need to. The creature—"

A low growl rumbled from the backseat.

"*Peaches*," I said. "I don't think he likes to be called 'the creature.'"

"Fine, *Peaches* has some interesting qualities that I think will be useful. Wait, what did you say about containing?"

"Yeah, stronger runes for containing anyone who comes to the office without an invitation. Why?"

"If you were Chaos and needed to contain someone

powerful, supernatural, how would you do it?" Monty asked.

"You mean if I were an old god and needed to stop Charon from doing his job without anyone else noticing?" I asked.

"Chaos is a lesser god," Monty said. "He's powerful but not on the same level as, say, Hades for example. He would need to put the Ferryman somewhere secure."

"But how?" I asked. "You don't just roll up in a van, toss Charon in the back, and drive to a supernatural black site."

"No, you kill a sorcerer where you'd want Charon to show up and then trap him there."

"That would mean that Chaos knew the Ferryman was taking sorcerer souls or whatever it is sorcerers have when they die," I said. "It means Hades has a leak. Unless Chaos and Hades are working together."

"Unlikely," Monty said, rubbing his chin. "Hades said Charon had been tasked with sorcerer deaths. We need to know who else knew about that."

I got off on the next exit at Canal Street and jumped back on the Westside Highway heading downtown.

"What are you doing?" Monty asked. "Where are we going?"

"No time like the present," I said. "Let's go ask him."

"If we're right and Chaos knew about the Ferryman's new assignment, he would have to find a place to detain him, somewhere secure," Monty said.

"The only place that would be strong enough to hold a being like Charon is—" I started.

"Haven," Monty finished.

"Shit, this complicates everything," I said.

"It means Roxanne was a target. As a Director, she would know who was placed in the detention wing."

"Chaos needed her out of the way before she noticed and spoke to you. We need to get to Haven."

I turned off the exit and headed down the street. One World Plaza was two blocks away. A low growl rose from the back seat.

"Monty, stop molesting the dog," I said. "He doesn't like you much."

"I haven't even looked at the creature. Much less touch it."

The growl became louder and I pulled over to see what was irritating Peaches.

"You must have done something; he doesn't growl at me. We're bonded, remember?" I said with a smile as I got out of the car. "Did you cast one of those itching spells at him?"

"Of course, I want him to lose his mind in the car while you're doing what you call driving so we can have a collision and all die in a fiery crash," Monty replied. "Obviously my life is too dull and needs some excitement."

I was in the back seat searching next to Peaches when he barked and tried to destroy my left eardrum. I staggered out of the car, rubbing my ear.

"A little warning next time would be great," I said as thunder filled the night and the top of One World Plaza exploded. I looked up and saw the ten floors occupied by Terra Sur Global were on fire.

TWENTY-THREE

I PRESSED THE speed dial for Ramirez. He picked up after the second ring.

"Bad news," I said.

"Every time you call it's bad news. What is it this time?"

"You have a situation," I said, looking up at the inferno. "It's not terrorists, so NYTF needs to be lead on this. Any development on MoMA?"

"I don't have your inventory yet," he said. "The museum is trying to hold the NYTF liable for the damages. You can imagine how well that's going."

"You need to get downtown now. One New York Plaza."

"And where are you?" he asked.

"Same place. Bring firetrucks and ambulances."

"Why am I not surprised? Shit, on my way," he said and hung up.

I ran to the lobby entrance but it was empty. I tried the door and it opened. There was no one behind the reception desk and none of the security was present. Debris littered the lobby and most of the windows were shattered. Monty walked up behind me.

"What are you looking for?" Monty asked. "There's no one here. Procedure would have them evacuate the building in case of something like this."

We stood next to the massive reception desk. The waiting area was destroyed. I could see small fires starting in several parts of the lobby.

"This was Chaos," I said. "I can feel it; he's close."

"I agree, but would he be insane enough to be in the lobby of the building he just exploded?" Monty said. "Only a psychopathic megalomaniac bent on destruction would behave in that manner."

"That would be offensive if it weren't true," a voice said from behind us. "Hello, gentlemen."

Chaos.

"Where's Roxanne?" Monty said and flung a bright red orb of fire at him.

Chaos caught the orb and held it floating before him. He wore a white trench coat with a charcoal gray suit underneath. His hair was considerably longer since our last conversation. His eyes still did the creepy glowing thing. I saw the Infinite Amulet around his neck. Its gold face reflected the growing fires around us.

"I'd say a fireball in the face is rather rude," Chaos said, bouncing the orb in his hand. "Wouldn't you agree, Tristan?"

Judging from the surprise on Monty's face this was not normal. Chaos made a fist around the orb and it grew. I could feel the heat it gave off as I backed up into the large reception desk.

"Bloody hells," whispered Monty. "This would be a good time to run, Simon."

"Run where?" I answered. "Besides, we need that amulet."

"Here, let me give this back to you," Chaos said and released the orb of blue flame. It floated in front of him, bobbing in the air like a lazy bubble. He dropped his hand and flicked the orb back at us.

Monty made a gesture with his hands as I jumped back over the desk. There was a muffled explosion and Monty bounced off the wall and landed on the floor next to me, bruised and bloody.

"That didn't work," he groaned as he sat up. "He's a lot stronger than I imagined."

"No kidding," I hissed. "What gave it away— stopping the orb and playing catch with it, or making your mini inferno into a little ball of hell?"

"If you do as I ask, Tristan, I promise to kill her fast," Chaos said. "She won't suffer—much."

I drew Grim Whisper and stood, taking aim at his center mass, and emptied the magazine. I managed to put some excellent holes in his suit before I ducked behind the desk again.

"Runed ammunition?" Chaos said with a chuckle. "You're going to need more firepower than that."

"I left my RPG in my other jacket," I said, really wishing I had one as I looked at Monty. "We need to get an RPG with runed rockets."

"What do you say, Tristan?" Chaos asked, getting closer as I heard his feet crunch glass. "I'm really here for you. Exploding Hades and his building was just a pleasant distraction."

"While that offer sounds tempting, I think I'll pass," Monty yelled in response. He traced runes as he looked at me. "This spell will obliterate the entire lobby and everything in it."

"Including him?" I asked, pointing behind me at Chaos. "Tell me this plan includes him."

"That's the plan," Monty said. "When I say, you head for that window"— he pointed down the desk to a window at the far end that was shattered by debris —"and don't look back."

"Where will you be?" I said.

"Right behind you," he answered. "Go!"

I ran down the length of the desk and made it to the window. I turned to see Monty stand up, raise his arm above his head, and cast the spell. Hundreds of black orbs escaped his hand and flew off in every direction. Chaos threw up a shield and ran at him.

Monty made no move to join me so I did the only sensible thing. I pressed the large bead on the mala and ran back in. Monty saw me and shook his head as he brought his arm down. The last thing I saw was Chaos crashing into Monty, and then everything went white.

TWENTY-FOUR

"WE MAY NEED to tranquilize that thing," a voice said in the distance. "We can't get close to the body. What kind of breed is that anyway? Looks like some sort of hellhound."

I cracked open a bruised eye to see Peaches standing over me in full 'tear you to shreds' mode. He straddled my body and gave off a low rumble that resembled a jackhammer.

"Good dog," I said, petting him behind the ears. He looked at me for a few seconds as if assessing my general health. He seemed satisfied with my state of near death and stepped over me. He moved a few inches to my side and sat on his haunches. I saw Ramirez talking to some of the other NYTF officers and motioned for him to get closer. He approached me cautiously, keeping an eye on Peaches.

"When did you get—I want to say a dog, but that animal hardly qualifies," he said. "What is that?"

"Monty," I said, looking at the destroyed lobby.

"Monty is in there."

I tried to stand up but the ground tilted under me. Ramirez put a hand on my shoulder and quickly removed it as Peaches growled to let him know it was bad idea to touch me.

We were across the street from One World Plaza. The building was a nightmare. The lobby was gutted, with fires blazing everywhere. The top floors were also in flames and debris was falling all around the building.

"We haven't found him yet," Ramirez said, his voice grim. "Once the fire is under control we'll go in, I promise."

I pushed him away and stood shakily. Peaches walked next to me as I limped across the street. I stood near one of the blown-out windows of the lobby.

"Strong!" Ramirez yelled. "You can't go in there!"

"Hell I can't. Peaches, stay," I said and pressed the mala.

Nothing happened.

I pressed it again and nothing. No shield appeared. I got as close as possible to the fire. Two firefighters were running in my direction, most likely to 'escort' me to a safe distance. I stepped even closer.

I leaned against a column to regain my balance and pressed the mark. The world grew out of focus and I entered the lobby. The fire was raging mostly near the desk and the far walls. I managed to keep my distance from the flames and walked around. I saw no sign of Monty or Chaos. I walked back to where Peaches was sitting and time snapped back to its normal flow.

"We need to get you out of here now, sir, it's not safe," one of the firefighters said as he approached.

"Please, come with me."

Ramirez walked up and grabbed my arm.

"I got him," he said to the firefighter and showed him his badge. "He's with me."

"Keep him away from the 3D zone," the firefighter said. "I don't know how many deaths we have. I don't want to add another."

"I got it," Ramirez said and pulled me to one of the ambulances on the scene He got the attention of one of the EMTs. "Check him out. He was near the explosion."

Ramirez waited nearby with Peaches, watching me as the EMT examined me. He stepped away when some NYTF investigators called him over.

"Don't leave without speaking to me," he said as he walked. "I mean it."

I nodded and waited for him to walk off before gathering my things.

The EMT gave me a onceover. I knew what he would find—nothing. My body was dealing with the effects of the explosion and repairing any damage. The look on the EMT's face was a mixture of fascination and revulsion as cuts closed and my skin returned to normal.

"What the hell are you?" he whispered, moving away from me. "You're not normal."

"Cursed is the word you're looking for," I said and jumped out of the ambulance. "Peaches, let's go."

I began walking to the Goat, with Peaches staying close. Ramirez caught up with me.

"Where are you going?" he asked with urgency. "Monty still hasn't been found."

"He's not in there," I said. "You won't find any bodies in the lobby. I don't know about the top floors, though."

"How can you be sure? They haven't even put out the fire."

"The entity that attacked the building took him," I said.

"The entity? Who is it? Give me something," Ramirez said, and grabbed my arm. "Why would some entity take Tristan?"

"It was Chaos," I said. "Chaos took him."

Ramirez gave me a look of confusion. "What do you mean Chaos took him?"

"The god, Chaos—that is the entity that took him," I said and put my thumb on the driver's side door handle. "That's what we're facing."

Ramirez looked at the Goat as it did its clanging and unlocking. I opened the back door and Peaches jumped inside and settled on the back seat.

"*Coño*, Simon," Ramirez said and exhaled. "What are you going to do? You two are some of the toughest bastards I know, but going up against a *god* is way out of the NYTF's league."

"I know," I said, getting into the Goat. "I'm going to get some help and then I'm getting Monty back."

TWENTY-FIVE

THERE WAS ONLY one way I would get Chaos's attention. I needed to free the Ferryman, which meant breaking *into* Haven's detention center. Breaking *out* of a supernatural detention center is usually impossible.

The facilities were covered in redundant failsafes. I knew most of them used siphoning runes similar to what shutdown Monty in Hades's office. That prevented a supernatural assault. Sorcerers and high-level magic-users were stationed throughout the center. Some of them, like Roxanne, held positions in the center and could be called on in a moment's notice.

The only thing I had working in my favor was that I was breaking in, not out. Also, I doubted that the Ferryman would be on any registry of prisoners. It meant Chaos had someone on the inside helping him. It also meant that Charon would be kept away from the general population. In solitary or something similar.

I needed The Hack.

I drove back to the Moscow and left the car idling as

I entered with Peaches. Andrei took several steps back when he saw him.

"*Ad sobaka!* Helldog!" he said as he backed away.

Peaches stayed next to me and ignored him. I was focused on getting upstairs and getting equipped so I didn't pay Andrei much attention.

"Andrei," I said, "don't piss him off. He's a good dog—not a helldog, but he could probably rip off your arm. His name is Peaches."

"Peaches?" he asked, confused. "Like fruit?"

"Just not as sweet," I said. "Leave the car in front. I'll be right down."

"Fifteen minutes, then garage," he said, keeping an eye on Peaches.

That was ten minutes longer than usual. I would have to get Andrei something special for his birthday—maybe a slab of meat from the Rump.

I nodded as I headed for the stairs. I wasn't worried about Peaches because the Moscow was an animal-friendly building. Although if Olga saw him, she might consider changing the policy.

I approached the door to our office and punched in the code. The door unlocked with a click. I stayed outside because I knew Georgianna was still inside and probably a little twitchy after the Unfriendlies earlier visit.

"Georgianna, it's me," I said and looked down at Peaches. "And a guest."

"Open the door slowly," she said.

I heard the slide on a gun as I pushed the door open. Georgianna stood several feet back with one of the hand-cannons aimed at the door.

"Where did you get that?" I asked.

"Let me see your hand," she said. "Now."

I raised my right hand and looked down at the growling Peaches, who had moved into a 'pounce and destroy' pose when he saw a large weapon was pointed at me.

"Easy, boy," I whispered, and touched his head. "She's a friend."

"The *other* hand," she said, waving the cannon. "And turn it around."

I lifted my left hand and turned it around so that the palm faced me. A look of relief filled her face.

"It's you," she said and lowered the gun. Peaches sat up and remained still.

"Last time I checked," I said. "How did you know it was me? I could have been in disguise."

"As yourself? Your mark…it shimmers," she said. "Like a rainbow."

I looked at the endless knot but it looked plain to me. "Really? I don't see it."

She nodded.

"Where did you get that?" I asked warily.

"From one of the vampires in the kitchen," she said and put it on the table next to the sofa. "It's okay, Yama. It's really Simon."

From behind the door, I sensed Yama silently glide away. He carried a large staff called a bo. I recognized it from my practice with Master Yat. They were usually one or two inches thick.

The one he carried must have been the industrial Yama version. It looked about four inches thick and was covered in runes. He gave me a short nod and walked back to the kitchen to continue the cleanup.

"Good to see you up and about," I said. "Have a good nap?"

A grunt was my only reply. Yama—the master of eloquence.

"I'm guessing he wasn't holding that when the Unfriendlies dropped in for a visit," I said, looking at the bo.

I entered the space with Peaches next to me. Michiko's crew had done their work. I couldn't see any damage and the place looked great. Except for the dead vampire bodies. I would have to call Allen to remove them.

"Who?" she said. "You mean Colin?"

I nodded as I headed to my office. She padded noiselessly behind me. "I saw the Claddagh symbol," I said. "But they didn't seem too friendly."

"Oh, he's beautiful!" she exclaimed as she crouched to rub Peaches behind the ears. "Is he yours?"

"A gift," I said, looking down at the shameless dog as I opened the door to my office. "Supposed to help with office security, but I'm having my doubts."

"He's amazing. What's his name?"

"Peaches," I said with a straight face. I could tell she was avoiding the Colin topic.

"You're serious? It's not Rex or Midnight or something overly macho like Brutus?" she asked.

I shook my head. "Peaches. Want to share why they were so intent on giving you a barbeque? How did they get in, anyway?"

"That was my fault. I let them in. I didn't know Colin had joined the hit squad—he's my brother," she said after a pause. "They're after me because I'm allergic."

"I've never heard of allergies being a capital offense in vampire clans," I said as I walked over to the sidewall. "Then again I've never heard of allergic vampires. What are you allergic to?"

She remained silent as she rubbed Peaches some more. I placed my hand on a section of the wall and a panel slid back, revealing a large strongbox. I pulled it out and placed it on the desk next to the wall.

"I'm allergic to blood," she said.

"You're *what*? How can you be allergic to blood? You're a vampire. Wait, you can't drink any blood?"

She stood and I noted the defiant stance.

"I just am, okay? I can only drink AB-negative blood which is like one percent of the population."

Then it clicked. "The blood bank. They were getting a delivery of AB-negative."

She nodded. "I knew they were getting a shipment, I just didn't know they would be waiting for me," she said. "I wasn't thinking straight. I hadn't fed in days."

"So you've been shunned because you can only feed on AB-negative. Makes no sense. It's still blood and you're still a vampire."

"Vampire clans are pretty big on rules," she said. "My parents are okay with it, but the elders saw me as a threat to the clan and shunned me."

I put my hands on the strongbox and took a few deep breaths.

"Hey, where's Tristan?" she asked, looking around. "Is he coming?"

"Tristan—is in trouble," I said. "Someone—

something— dangerous took him and I'm going to get him back."

"Alone?" she asked. "Can I help?"

"I'm working on that part," I said and looked down at the strongbox. "Don't think you can come with me. If something happened to you, Chi would do her best to kill me—repeatedly."

"Are you two a couple or something?" she asked and blushed. "I mean, I can tell you have feelings for her."

"It's something, all right," I said with a tight smile, "just don't know what."

"What's in the box?"

"A way to get help," I said and opened it.

TWENTY-SIX

MONTY ALWAYS BELIEVED in preparation. He always said a prepared mage is an effective mage. I looked down into the rune-covered, lead-lined strongbox and exhaled. Black wisps of smoke floated up from inside.

I focused and began removing the contents. Inside the box were several magazines of ammunition for the Grim Whisper. Grenades covered in runes sat next to the ammo.

"That looks dangerous," she said. "That smoke isn't helping, either."

"These are entropy rounds," I said, removing the magazines carefully. "Monty made them for me in case I came up against something I couldn't handle, or he was—"

"Dead?" she finished.

I nodded. "He made these powerful enough to stop a renegade sorcerer or mage."

"Did he mean himself? Was this in case he went out

of control?"

"If you had asked me that last week, I would have said no. Now I'm not so sure."

"Does a sorcerer have Tristan?"

"No, something worse—something stronger. A god who wants to destroy everything."

"Shit," she said. "This is bad."

I began filling my pockets with the extra magazines. I grabbed the runed grenades and put them in another pocket.

"Is that going to be enough?"

"I don't know if they will work on a god," I said. "But I have one more thing I think will work."

"You don't have a rocket launcher or something like that?"

"It's on my to-do list right after getting back alive," I said. "Sunrise is in a few hours. I need you to stay here with Peaches and keep the office secure."

I put the strongbox back and sealed the wall. I grabbed the laptop from my desk and headed to the kitchen to grab something quick to eat because facing an insane god on an empty stomach is just bad policy. I needed to get Charon out of the detention center, but first I was going to need more firepower.

I headed for the door after eating a few sandwiches, and Peaches walked up to me. I rubbed his ears as he sat on his haunches and looked up at me.

"Stay here with Georgianna and keep the place secure, boy," I said, not knowing how much he understood. He barked and walked over to stand next to Georgianna.

"If I don't come back—" I started.

"You'll be back," she said as she rubbed Peaches. "Make sure you bring Tristan back too."

"That's the plan," I said and headed out. I heard her lock and secure the door as I took the stairs down. I pulled out my phone and called The Hack.

The call took a few moments as it bounced across several sites and then piggybacked on another line in a backhaul. From there it jumped to a T3 line and rerouted the call, repeating the process several times. Hack tried to explain it to me one time. All I got was that it made it impossible to trace the call.

He picked up after a long silence.

"Simon, situation is getting critical," he said. "MoMA got sliced and One New York Plaza got flamed. You in the loop on this?"

Half the time I barely grasped what he was saying but fortunately for me he occasionally would translate into English I understood.

"Go light on the hackspeech. I need schematics to the New York Detention Center on 1st Avenue between 37th and 38th Streets," I said. "Specifically, points of egress that would allow me to get in undetected."

I heard the typing of keys as I descended the stairs into the lobby. Andrei stood by the entrance with a concerned look on his face. I guessed he was still rattled by Peaches' entrance. I gave him a quick nod, stepped outside, into the Purple Goat, when The Hack got back on the line.

"Hard way or easy way?" he said.

"Easy way," I said. "Preferably one that avoids magic-users and security on site."

"Easy way is to sneak in with food staff on the shift rotation at six a.m.," he replied. "Get in through loading to the kitchen. Less security at that time. Schematics and schedule rotation sent to your laptop."

I opened my laptop and placed it next to me on the passenger seat. After several clicks, I was looking at a cross section of the detention center complete with a schedule and personnel list. I would have to enter from the back on the 38th Street side through one of the loading docks.

"I can manage that. Can you check if they have any prisoners they are trying to hide? Something off-grid but high-level."

"A prisoner they want to keep as a mirage? One sec." More keys clicking and some low whistling.

"What'd you find?" I asked. "And where?"

"Sub-level four, northwest block, cell seven," he said with a hint of admiration. "You'll need an elite strike unit, with loads and loads of ammo. You may also want a sorcerer or two. Just for insurance."

"That bad?" I asked and winced. "Any idea who they have in that cell? Did you say sub-level four? Since when?"

"Yep, the bowels of the beast. Not drawn on any schematics, means an unofficial site," he said. "Prisoner is unregistered, but high-level enough to rotate two sorcerers and a squad of commandos off normal duty and assign them there. You going solo?"

"I have to—Monty is MIA and the only one who can help me I'm hoping is in that cell."

"You're my new hero," he said. "It looks suicidal, but that's your forte. Anything else? This connection is getting hot."

"That's it, thanks for everything, Hack," I said. "Don't know if this is a roundtrip."

"I hear you. If not, I'll meet you on the other side. Remember it's all tombyards and butterflies." He had hung up before I could ask him what he meant. Typical hackspeech.

I was reasonably certain I could get into the detention center. Getting out was another thing entirely. I had one more call to make, and if he didn't agree, Monty was as good as dead.

I dialed Ramirez.

TWENTY-SEVEN

"YOU WANT WHAT?" he yelled. "Are you out of your mind? And you're going to do what?"

"I need to use the negation rune to defeat Chaos," I said.

"No, no, the other part, where you break into the detention center—break *into* it—and free a prisoner from sub-level four. I didn't even know they had a sub-level four, Simon."

"Me either, but I'm guessing that's where the Ferryman is being held."

"You're guessing? You don't have positive ID on the prisoner in this cell?"

"How do you think I should go about getting that, Ramirez? The level doesn't officially exist. Should I just go ask them if I can peek in the cell?"

"Shit, why are you telling me this? You know I can't help you," he said. "You're putting your hand in a blender and expecting it to leave you with all your fingers."

"I need the rune. Once I get out—"

"If you get out," he said. "This is suicide."

"*Once* I get out, I have to get Monty. He knows how to use the rune."

"Get Monty? What do you mean *get* Monty? Where's Tristan?"

"Chaos has him. And I'm going to get him back."

"Fine, you're going to do this—I'll give you the rune on one condition: I come along. If you say no, kiss the rune goodbye."

"Ramirez, you don't know what we're dealing with here. Chaos isn't a rabid werewolf we can cuff," I said. "Silver restraints aren't going to work on him."

"Tick-tock, Simon," he replied. "Six a.m. shift change is coming soon and I can get you in easier with my credentials."

"Goddammit, Ramirez," I said, exasperated. "Meet me at the Center in twenty."

"I love it when you talk dirty to me," he said and hung up.

He was right about making it easier for me to get inside. It also meant it was easier to get him killed. Once I had the rune, I would find a way to make sure he was safe but out of the way.

I drove up the West Side Highway and cut across 34th Street until I was on 1st Avenue. I arrived at 38th Street in fifteen minutes and dialed Ramirez again.

"Where are you?" I asked when he picked up.

"Down the street. We can't go in the front door even with my credentials. The kitchen idea is a good one."

I drove down the block until I saw the NYTF cruiser. The only way it could have been more conspicuous is if he painted NYTF in neon orange on the side.

"Good thing you decided to come in under the radar," I said as I walked over to his vehicle. "This doesn't say NYTF at all."

"Ha ha, hilarious. You and Tristan should go on the road."

He walked to the rear, lifted the hatch of the cruiser, and I noticed two large duffel bags in rear seat. He pulled out one of them and handed me the other. Next to both of them sat the case holding the negation rune.

"Well, my regular car was sliced in two. You might remember it from your little visit to the museum," he said. "I had to borrow this from the motor pool."

I hefted the bag in my hand. "What's in here?" I asked. The weight indicated weapons and an enormous amount of spare ammo.

"What do you think? You want to visit the unauthorized level of a maximum detention center. I'm not bringing sandwiches and soda."

"About that—" I started.

"*Hombre*, don't waste your breath. I'm coming with you," he said. "You get the rune when we get back out here."

"I think it would be better if you gave it to me now," I said, looking at the case in the cruiser. "That way it will be safe."

"Nice try," he said. "As soon as I give it to you, I get left behind. You need help."

"I don't want to see you dead, Ramirez," I said. "This is going to be a gauntlet. I know the NYTF deals with some insane shit, but take that and dial it to eleven. That's what's waiting for us. I don't even know if this falls under your jurisdiction."

"Doesn't matter. They put a black site *inside* my city. I'm *making* it my jurisdiction."

"These guys shoot first and ask questions later," I said as we walked back to the Goat. "Later meaning never."

"That's why I came prepared," he said, and tossed his bag at my feet. He went to the back of the cruiser, grabbed the rune case, and handed it to me.

"My guess is you don't know how to use this. This is all that sorcery stuff Tristan does, right?"

"Ramirez," I said, my voice tight, "don't ever let him hear you call him a sorcerer—ever."

"Sorry. What is he, really? A wizard?" he asked. "We don't get debriefed on the levels of magic use in the NYTF, you know. Most of the guys just think Tristan is insane and dangerous."

"Wizard? No, you're thinking Chicago or St. Louis. Monty is a mage and yes, he's dangerous. Probably a little insane too."

"Which makes you just as unstable."

"You already knew that," I said, smiling.

"And he knows how to use this rune? I mean, really use it?"

I nodded. "That's totally Monty," I said. "I deal with bullets and blades."

"That—I can understand," he said. "Put the rune in your grape-mobile. I heard the locks on it. Sounds pretty secure."

I took the case and put it in the trunk. It was almost as large as the trunk on the Phantom. I placed my hand on the handle and secured the Goat.

"It's not a grape-mobile, it's the Goat," I said, running my hand along the side of it.

"Yeah, sure, they didn't have another color?" he said, looking at his watch. "We have twenty minutes before the shift change. What's the play?"

"We go in through the kitchen and make our way down to sub-level four," I said. "Once there we have to head to the northwest block, cell seven."

I showed him the schematic and he narrowed his eyes as he analyzed it.

"It looks like only one elevator goes down that far. No stairs. Where did you get these plans? This is a top secret document."

"I think you're overreacting. How do you know it's top secret?" I said.

"The words 'Top Secret' across the top are not a suggestion," he answered, pointing at the screen. "You need to delete this file."

"It auto-erases in a few minutes," I said, closing the laptop. "You have the route?"

He nodded. "The elevator is going to be a problem. Most likely has some kind of security pass."

"Even guys on sub-level four have to eat," I said, putting the laptop in the Goat and locking the door. "Someone on staff has to have access."

We walked up the street to the rear of the detention center. The imposing gray building covered over half the block. Its darker color gave the impression of being in shadow to the hospital, which was constructed using white brick. It stood fifteen stories, the same as the hospital wing, but with an extra dose of ominous.

"I thought these buildings were connected?" Ramirez asked, looking up. "Would make our lives easier if we could go in through the hospital wing."

"When they first designed this place, they were. It was a good idea—at first. Then a sorcerer broke out of the detention center and made it to the hospital wing."

"What happened?" he asked.

"It was a nightmare. He managed to get to pediatrics before they dropped him."

"Shit," Ramirez said, shaking his head with a hiss. "He went after the kids?"

I nodded. "Ever since then they destroyed any connecting passages to maintain security. Over there," I said and pointed to the growing crowd entering the building.

We walked into the loading dock and joined the shift change going into the kitchen. When we got to the security checkpoint, Ramirez handed him his badge and spoke to the officer on duty. I read the name Gregory on his badge.

Tall, about two-hundred and fifty pounds, he looked like he hit the gym regularly and punished the weights while there. His blue eyes were sharp and darted over us quickly. They lingered over the bags for a few seconds before returning to the credentials in his hands. Everything about him screamed ex-military. It only meant the detention center took their security seriously.

"We need to check on one of the inmates," Ramirez said, putting his wallet away and handing me mine. "Sub-level two."

"At six a.m.?" Gregory asked, looking unconvinced.

"Isn't that a little early for an inspection, sir?"

"Brass is busting my ass about this," Ramirez answered with a rueful grin. "They aren't supposed to know we're coming. You want to call it in?"

"Which means more paperwork for me at the end of shift—no thanks," Gregory said. "You know where you're going or do I need to call you an escort?"

"We got it, thanks," Ramirez answered, picking up his bag. "Those elevators over there should lead us to sub-level two."

"Last bank on the left," Gregory said, pointing.

The morning shift had finished checking in, leaving just us two at the security checkpoint. Everyone was headed to their respective stations. We made to follow them in when Officer Gregory cleared his throat.

"What's in the bags?" he asked, resting a hand on the holster at his side. "I'm going to need to see what's in them—. Sorry, sir, regulations."

"No, I understand, rules are rules," Ramirez answered and gave me a quick look. "Stay there, I'll bring them to you."

Ramirez grabbed my bag, walked over to the security booth, and turned his back to the camera. As Gregory leaned over to examine the bag, Ramirez stepped close. The next moment, I saw Gregory slump forward. Ramirez caught him before his head hit the desk and helped him back into his chair.

Ramirez grabbed the bags, handed me one and headed for the elevators.

"Did you—?"

He gave me a surprised look and showed me a small rectangular device he held in his palm. It had two prongs on one end and a large battery on the other.

"I just gave him a mild shock. He'll be out for a bit. I don't make a habit of killing friendlies, Simon."

"He's as big as a house, so that must be some Taser," I said. "You sure you didn't stop his heart?"

"It's an N-Taser. Shuts the brain down but avoids damage to the heart. At least that's how Jhon, our Q-master, explained it."

"Oh, so you just gave him brain damage. Much better. "How long is he out for?"

"We have about an hour before he starts to regain consciousness," Ramirez replied as the elevator doors opened. "I suggest we focus on the task at hand."

We stepped inside. I looked at the panel but saw no button for a sub-level four.

"What the hell?" I said, and looked outside. "It must be another elevator."

TWENTY-EIGHT

"WAIT," RAMIREZ SAID, putting his bag down. "Hold the door."

He ran back to the security booth as I placed a foot in the door track, preventing the doors from closing. He came back holding a key card.

"There's nowhere to put that," I said as I searched the panel. "We need another elevator."

"Not according to the schematics. This is the only one that goes to sub-level four."

"Except that there's no button or slot or anything," I said, frustration evident in my voice.

"It's a secret floor," he said and placed the key card against the panel under the sub-level three button. The panel lit up briefly and the doors closed. "They aren't going to make it obvious."

"How did you know?" I asked.

"I've been around my share of black sites. It's always something clever, which only makes it predictable. We have about a minute—weapons check."

I tightened the straps holding the Ebonsoul to my upper thigh and made sure the Grim Whisper was ready with one in the chamber. I hoped the mala's shield worked, but I wasn't depending on it.

"Ramirez, if you see me take damage, don't stop," I said.

I didn't know how to tell him about my curse and this wasn't exactly the moment to say—'Hey, by the way, I'm cursed and I don't think I can die,'" so I lied.

"What do you mean don't stop? I'm not leaving you down there."

"I'll be able to take the damage. Monty runed my coat to be better than armor," I said. "I'm good, so just get to the cell."

He shook his head in disbelief and checked his weapons.

"Both of you are lunatics," he said.

"Just let me deal with the sorcerers."

The elevator doors whispered open and I took a quick glance down the hall before ducking my head back inside. The floor was empty. Ramirez unzipped his bag, walked out of the elevator and strode down the hallway.

"What are you doing?" I whispered as I caught up with him.

"Best way to infiltrate a location is to act like you belong there," he replied.

The level was a large rectangle with three massive cell doors in each of the four sides. A right turn at the end of the hallway put us facing another row of cells.

"Halt!" a voice from behind us said. "Present your ID or I will fire."

We turned and Ramirez slowly put his hand into an inside pocket to pull out his badge. The guard stood ten yards away with his gun drawn. It was clear he swam in the same gene pool as Gregory upstairs. He was easily over six-foot-two and tipping the scales approaching three-hundred pounds of mostly muscle.

"Lieutenant Angel Ramirez, NYTF, and I'm here because someone reported a disturbance," Ramirez said as he dropped his bag. "Can you direct me to your supervisor? We seemed to be turned around."

"Bullshit," the guard answered. "You two just got off on the wrong floor."

He grabbed his shoulder radio.

"I have two intru—" he started.

Ramirez fired twice. The first shot exploded the radio. The second shot hit the guard's center mass and propelled him down the hallway and into the wall. A small crater erupted behind him as he smashed into the wall with force and crumpled to the ground. We ran to his body and dragged him to the elevator bank.

"Kinetic rounds? Since when does the NYTF use those?" I asked, surprised.

"Since we aren't here to kill everyone. What are you carrying?"

"Entropy rounds," I said after a pause. "For Chaos."

He narrowed his eyes at me and shook his head.

"Are you crazy? You hit one of these guys with one of those and they're gone," he said. "Bringing a nuke to a gun fight."

I grabbed him by the shoulder. "I'm not here to negotiate or ask for cooperation."

"I'm not here to massacre a bunch of guys just

doing their jobs, either," he answered and shook my hand off his shoulder. "Even if this whole level is unauthorized."

"That's why you're doing the shooting," I answered, looking at the doors. "Cell seven must be back around the corner."

"That way," he said and gestured forward. "Get a move on, Simon."

"I'm kind of surprised there aren't more guards," I said as we turned the corner.

"You mean like that?" Ramirez said as he pointed ahead of us.

Down the hallway, a squad of commandos in battle gear were headed in our direction.

"Light 'em up!" were the last words I heard before the gunfire erupted. We dived back around the corner as bullets filled the hallway, destroying the wall across from us.

"Guess they aren't going to ask for ID?" Ramirez said as he opened his bag.

"In about thirty seconds a group is going to come around behind us and then we're screwed," I said. "We need to neutralize them fast."

"I got this," he said and rummaged through his bag, pulling out several grenades. "These should do it."

"Kinetic grenades—NYTF is full of surprises. Those things are impossible to get."

"Not for me. I know a guy," he said and smiled. "You want to move down the hallway."

I ran down the corridor, keeping my eye on the distant corner. He crept up to the end of the hallway and tossed a handful of grenades at the commandos. I felt the wave of energy build as he ran back to my location. A blinding flash of light signaled the grenades going off. The explosion was silent, the screams weren't.

I was still seeing spots as I headed to the end of the corridor and I poked my head around to see the damage. Most of the commandos were down but alive. In the rear, I saw the real threat.

"There's a sorcerer back there," I said. "And he doesn't look like he wants to talk."

"Can I shoot him?" Ramirez asked. "Bouncing a person off a wall usually helps the conversation along."

"He just survived the grenades, so I don't think bullets are going to do much damage—at least not yours," I said.

"No alarms and no cameras," he said, looking around quickly. "They don't intend to capture us."

"Yeah, I noticed. It's a black site and we're trespassing. They can terminate with extreme prejudice. Pretty sure they don't want records of what happens down here."

"Sorcerer is all yours. I'll go around the other way and see if I can outflank and distract him," he said. "Are you going to be able to deal with the magic?"

"No choice," I said as I closed my jacket. "We need him alive, Angel. He may be the only way to open the cell door."

"Then don't kill him," he said and ran down the corridor away from me.

I turned the corner and stared at the fireball racing at me. There was no time to jump out of the way. I pressed the mala, but no shield appeared. I pulled out the Ebonsoul and prepared to be barbequed.

TWENTY-NINE

THE FIREBALL CRASHED into me. The heat caressed my body like a summer day. My immunity to magic didn't extend to my clothes. My runed coat managed not to burst into flame, but my jeans weren't so lucky. I put out the flames and ran at the surprised sorcerer.

He threw another fireball and I slid under it, feeling its heat as it flew over me. I closed the distance, stepping over unconscious commandos as I drew the Ebonsoul.

"I don't want to kill you, but you're beginning to piss me off," I said. "Enough with the fireballs."

He was a lanky mess. His robes barely fit and looked two sizes too large. His hair was disheveled and he had several days' worth of stubble on his face. I almost felt sorry for him, until I looked into his eyes. I was staring into the eyes of a killer.

He smiled, looked at me with a cold, dead expression, and pulled out a blade as long as the

Ebonsoul.

"You're immune to magic, but I'm sure you bleed like the rest of us," he said. "Tell your friend to stay back or I will burn all these men to ash."

He kept his voice low, but the menace punched me in the chest. I looked at the commandos in the hallway. There was no need for them to needlessly die.

"Ramirez, stay back—he's serious," I yelled. "I got this."

"All yours," Ramirez answered from around the corner. "Never liked magic anyway."

"I need you to open that cell door and let the prisoner out," I said. Monty had always said to try diplomacy first.

"Sure, right after you kill me," the sorcerer said, brandishing the blade.

So much for diplomacy.

The lesson I learned from Master Yat regarding fighting with knives and blades was twofold. Cut first, cut fast, or die. That and expect to be cut.

I stepped in and slashed across the horizontal, reversing direction at the last second and lunging. He skipped back and side-stepped my lunge while thrusting forward with his blade. I parried his thrust and hit him with a fist to the temple. He stepped back, dazed, as I kicked his knee and sent it sideways, shattering it and making sure he would have to use a cane for the rest of his life.

He fell, screaming and holding his leg. I placed a restraint on his wrist, neutralizing his magic, and kicked his blade away. Most sorcerers were too dependent on their abilities to learn how to fight properly without them. No one said you can't punch and kick in a knife fight.

"Open the door or I break the other one," I said as I crouched down next to him. I grabbed him by the arm and stood him up. I pushed him to the door as he fished out a black keycard. I saw the iridescent runes on its surface as he placed it against the wall next to the cell. The door hissed opened and slid away.

Ramirez came around the corner with his gun drawn.

"Is he cuffed?" he asked.

I nodded and handed him the second silver runic restraint while pocketing the keycard. "Put this on him and he should be easy to deal with."

Ramirez cuffed him and then placed what looked like a nicotine patch on the sorcerer's neck. The sorcerer collapsed a few seconds later.

"What was that?" I asked.

"Transdermal knockout patch," he answered as he started placing them on the commandos. "Go get your prisoner. I'll make sure they don't wake up for a few hours. Can I keep the restraints on him?"

I nodded. "Be right out," I said as I sheathed the Ebonsoul and stepped into the cell.

It was a large space—more living quarters than cell. A small table with a chair sat in one corner. On the opposite side of the room, I could see a bed. Directly across from that I saw a small sink, and adjacent to the sink was a door that I imagined led to a bathroom. Seated cross-legged in the middle of the floor was a man. He looked to be in his mid-thirties. His brown hair hung loosely to his shoulders. He wore a black T-shirt and black pants and was barefoot. Around the room, I saw runes inscribed on every surface. I couldn't make out what they meant, but I guessed they operated on the same principle as the restraints.

"Simon Strong, it is a pleasure," he said and gave me a short nod. "I really didn't expect *you*. But it makes sense."

"Charon?" I asked. "Are you the Ferryman?"

"Were you looking for someone else?" he said and stood. "Oh, I see."

His clothes transformed and shifted into a long robe with a cowl. "This better? Or do I need to escort a soul to prove my identity?"

"You have a lot of people wondering where you were," I asked as his clothes transformed back to the T-shirt and pants. "How did you manage that with all those runes?"

"Once you opened the door, you broke the seal," he said. "Shall we leave? Or are you here to join me?"

"I don't think we can go out the same way we came in. This level isn't supposed to exist."

"The elevators are all shutdown," Ramirez said from the doorway. "There may not be alarms blaring but you'd better believe they are coming for us."

Charon gave us a small smile. "You do realize there is no such thing as a locked room for me," he said. "I can travel anywhere at will."

"Well, except this one," I said, looking around. "This one seemed to stop you."

His face darkened for a moment as he nodded at me.

"Yes, this room is a trap, designed with runes unknown to man for millennia. Chaos lured me here with the soul of a sorcerer, and sealed me in."

"Can you take us right outside this building?" Ramirez asked. "I have some calls to make."

He gestured for us to come closer. I stepped closer but still kept my distance because, frankly, he was giving me a significant creepy vibe. He closed the distance and stood between Ramirez and me. He closed his eyes and everything went black.

THIRTY

WE STOOD OUTSIDE the detention center. I took two steps and felt my stomach twist into knots and the nausea hit me. The ground shifted and tilted sideways as I lost my balance. Ramirez and I doubled over and threw up our breakfasts.

"What did you do?" I asked in between retching and gasping.

"*Coño*, not even after my worst hangovers have I felt like this," Ramirez said and leaned on a parked car. "What happened?"

Charon walked over to where we were redecorating the sidewalk. He was no longer barefoot, now wearing a black suit with a white shirt and deep-blue tie.

"My method of travel can have some unpleasant side-effects. My apologies," he said, keeping his distance from the both of us. "The discomfort should pass momentarily."

I started walking to the Goat, not wanting to remain in front of the detention center longer than we had to.

I placed my hand on the handle and unlocked the door.

"Is Monty alive?" I asked as I opened the door. "Can you tell?"

"I don't deal in life—I deal in death," Charon said. "Are you referring to Tristan Montague?"

I nodded and regretted the action immediately as the horizon swam before me. "Can you tell if he's alive or at least not dead?" I asked and held down more retching.

"I'm not omniscient," Charon said. "I only know when someone dies. In this current iteration, my purpose is to gather the souls of recently deceased sorcerers. Tristan is not a sorcerer."

"How about locating him?" I asked, once my stomach stopped doing somersaults. "Can you sense where he may be?"

"Simon," Ramirez said, putting a hand on my shoulder, "there's a good chance Tristan is dead."

"I didn't ask for your opinion." I shrugged off his hand, and then it hit me. "Charon, can you tell me where the last sorcerer died, a soul you didn't collect because of your being trapped?"

He closed his eyes for a moment and tilted his head up.

"There," he said and pointed. "There is an eight-sided structure several miles from here surrounded by water. That soul is currently enthralled and can't be escorted."

I looked in the direction he pointed. The only place that fit the description didn't make sense, though.

"Are you certain?" I asked. "That's Roosevelt Island. It's all luxury buildings and Cornell University. Why would Chaos pick that location?"

"That is where he is and I must return to Hades to report." Nine sorcerer souls have been taken in my absence and I must restore balance."

"Hades? His building was destroyed by Chaos. I don't know if he made it."

"Hades is nearly impossible to destroy, much like Chaos," he said. "You can't kill chaos."

"He's immortal?" Ramirez asked, surprised. "Simon, this is a bad idea."

"The concept of chaos may be immortal; the body he resides in isn't," Charon answered. "I said nearly impossible. The body he inhabits can be killed, but not without great effort. He is a god, after all."

"Chaos wants to weaponize the null rune, so how do I stop him? He's going to kill Roxanne and Monty."

"Considering your current state,"—Charon looked at Ramirez briefly before turning back to me—"I would say you have the greatest chance of stopping him. Use the tools you have at hand."

"What tools? My sword can't scratch him and I don't know if entropy rounds will work on a god," I said. "I can't beat him."

"They don't need to work on a *god*, Simon. Chaos shares your affliction. I must go."

He stepped back, closed his eyes for a few seconds, and disappeared.

"Well, that wasn't cryptic at all," I said. "Ramirez, I'm taking the negation rune."

He nodded. "Listen, Simon, why not just locate this bastard, Chaos, and call in the magical cavalry and bomb the place?" he said.

"What if Monty is alive? Besides, there is no 'magical cavalry.' Monty is the only mage I know."

"That's a big if," he said.

"He would come for me no matter what. That 'if' would be enough. That's what we do. It's who we are," I said. "He's my friend. He's family."

"Okay, what time do we leave?" he asked.

"*We* don't do anything. You need to shut this place down or at least inform someone on the NYTF you trust about this black site."

"That's a short list," he said.

"Take this," I said and handed him the black runed-covered keycard.

"What's this?"

"That's the key to the cells on sub-level four, in case you need proof that the level exists," I said. "Shut it down."

"You can't go there alone, Simon."

"I'm not alone. Monty is alive. I just need to get him this rune and we can finish this."

"This Chaos god will try to kill you," Ramirez said. "Don't let him."

I looked down at my mark and nodded. "It's possible, but I have to try. If I don't go, he'll kill Monty and turn the null rune into a weapon, which means we all die."

"Be careful, *pendejo*," he said as I jumped into the Goat. "You still owe me dinner and I'm collecting when you get back."

I lowered the window and gave him my single-finger salute. His laughter followed me down the street and I realized it was probably the last time I would hear it.

THIRTY-ONE

I WAS CROSSING the 59th Street Bridge when I felt the cool metal against the back of my head. I glanced into the rear-view mirror. The surprise almost caused me to lose control of the Goat. It was Corbel.

"You want to focus on the road," he whispered, holding the gun steady. "Would hate to have to kill you twice."

"I see you took my advice about deodorant," I said, trying to keep my voice even. "How the hell did you make it? How did you get past the runes on the Goat?"

"I work for a *god*, Strong. Tristan's runes were about as complicated as a Rubik's cube."

"You know, those things can be challenging. I still haven't solved one."

"Why did you do it?" he asked his voice hard. "Hades is a hard-ass but he actually helped you and you repay him with exploding his office? Good people died."

"Do what? What are you talking about?" I asked,

confused.

"I'm still trying to figure out how you managed to plant the explosives," he said. "The building's security should have spotted you."

"That's because it wasn't me. Chaos rigged that explosion."

"Chaos, as in the *god* Chaos?" he said. "Bullshit. Hades banished him from this plane centuries ago."

"Well, it didn't stick. Chaos is here, with a grudge, and is going to weaponize a null rune."

"He can't do anything with a null rune unless he has an Infinite Amulet," Corbel said and grew silent when I didn't answer. "He has an Infinite Amulet, doesn't he?"

I nodded. "Relic from the war. Stolen from the museum."

"Of course it was—shit, you people are stupid," he said, sitting back and removing the gun from the back of my head. "Where's your partner, the smart one, Tristan?"

"Chaos took him—needs him, rather his blood—to complete the ritual," I said. "They're on Roosevelt Island in some eight-sided building."

"The Octagon," Corbel said. "Used to be the main entrance to the New York City lunatic asylum back in the 1800s. That's about the only thing that makes sense."

"Why?" I asked, trying not to look in the rear-view mirror.

"An asylum is the perfect place for Chaos. It still holds the residual energies of the people that were housed there. He will use that to get stronger."

"That was almost two hundred years ago," I said.

"How can there still be energies there?"

"Two hundred years is not even a blink when you measure your life in millennia. Trust me on this."

"Do you know how to stop him?" I asked. "Does Chaos have a weakness?"

"Stop him? Is that what you are planning on doing with your gun and knife?"

"He has Monty."

"Who's probably dead by now. The only reason we are still alive is because the ritual must be done at night. He only needs the sorcerer essences and the mage blood."

"Which he has," I said. "He killed nine sorcerers while Charon was trapped. He still has one left to kill."

"Like I said, probably dead by now," he said. "Want my advice?"

"Not really," I said as I pulled off the bridge exit into Queens.

"Get out of the city while you still can. Maybe he will lose interest and kill you last."

I pulled over and stopped the Goat.

"You should really consider motivational speaking. You have a gift."

"Call it like it is," he said, holstering his gun. "You know why he picked Roosevelt Island, besides the Octagon?"

"I'm guessing it wasn't for a view of the skyline."

"Ha ha, no," he said. "When that rune is first activated, it sends out a pulse wave that disables everything and everyone magical in a ten-mile radius. It's like a magical EMP."

"That's the entire city," I whispered, looking out at

the semi-dark skyline of Manhattan. "No one will be able to stop him."

"Not in time," Corbel answered. "By the time someone does come it will be too late. After that pulse, the amulet is charged. He will have a weapon that can undo reality with a thought."

"Whoever thought this amulet was a good idea deserves a swift kick in the nuts. With steel-toed boots."

"You can ask your friend Tristan about that," he said and stepped out of the Goat. "If I were you I would forget about taking on Chaos and find someplace to ride this out."

"Really, and where do you suggest?" I asked. "You know a safe-house around here?"

"Well, for you, the only safe place is the one you can't go to," he said and started walking away.

"Where is that?" I asked, knowing the answer.

"Death— he won't follow you there," he answered and disappeared around a corner.

THIRTY-TWO

I CROSSED THE Roosevelt Island Bridge, making it onto the island with little trouble. The one main street was deserted and the island appeared empty. I figured if Chaos had nine sorcerers, they would be protecting the Octagon until after the ritual was completed. It was still midafternoon and I had to formulate a plan besides the 'run in and die' one I had.

I parked the Goat just on the other side of the bridge, locked it, and walked north toward the Octagon, which was now converted to the main entrance of a deserted apartment complex.

I carried the case with the negation rune and kept to the shadows. I'd never visited the island. It always felt off to me somehow. Tonight that feeling was reinforced by the fact that Chaos had chosen it to complete the ritual.

"So you plan on just walking in?" a voice whispered in my ear. "Maybe asking Chaos to return your friend nicely?"

"Goddammit, Corbel, I almost buried my blade in your chest," I hissed as I tried to calm my racing heart. "What are you doing here? You told me to run."

"If you didn't sense me, you need more training," he whispered. "Hades helped you—for some reason I still can't understand—but I don't want to have to tell him I let you fail alone."

"Hades is dead. Chaos took out the top ten floors of the building."

"A little explosion like that isn't going to kill him," he replied as he shifted closer to the wall of the building. "He's probably sitting in some restaurant having dinner right now."

"Can you call him?" I asked. "We could use the backup."

"No, and before you ask, he won't get involved. Not unless it threatens him directly."

"A null rune turned into a weapon doesn't threaten him directly?"

"Hades is one of the three: unless it's going to erase the planet—they don't care. I'm still amazed he gave you the pup," Corbel said. "He must really think you're special or just need a lot of help. I'm leaning toward the latter."

"Almost sounded like a compliment, thanks," I said.

"What's your plan? Once it's nightfall, he'll start the ritual with killing the last sorcerer and your friend."

"He has nine sorcerers according to Charon. I need to disable them, get the negation rune to Monty, and strip Chaos of the null rune before he kills Roxanne and completes the ritual."

He looked at me as if I had just uttered nonsense.

"I *know* what you have to do, but that's not what I asked you. I asked you *how* you were going to do it?"

"I'm immune to magic so I can handle whatever the sorcerers throw at me."

"Are you immune to bullets? Do you know if they're armed?"

"I'm assuming they are, which is why I brought entropy rounds."

"How did you get your hands on entropy ammo? You have a gun that can fire entropy rounds?"

I showed him the Grim Whisper, and he nodded. "Monty made it and the ammunition," I said as black smoke drifted up from the gun.

"I'm beginning to see why Hades is helping you. That ammo is overkill for sorcerers when normal bullets will do. I don't see a silencer. The first shot will bring everyone to us."

"Every round it fires is silenced and I have enough for both," I said. "I'm not here to negotiate. He has my friend and I'm getting him back—alive."

"Sun's going down. Better get this started sooner rather than later, then. I doubt they'll be expecting an attack. We take down the outer perimeter and then enter the Octagon. If we find Tristan alive we have a chance—"

"*When* we find him alive," I said. "What weapon are you using?"

"I'm known as the 'Hound of Hades' for a reason. I don't need a weapon, Strong."

We came around the corner of the apartment complex and stuck to the shadows. On our right was the building parking lot. I could make out tennis courts on the other side of the lot.

Outside the Octagon, I saw two sorcerers standing guard and looking bored. Corbel shifted off to my right and disappeared. I drew Grim Whisper and dropped the first one. The entropy round acted like a hollow-point bullet. Instead of the bullet expanding, it expanded nothingness on impact. A whirlwind of energy surrounded the sorcerer and he disappeared a second later.

I barely had time to react when a blast of air knocked me on my back. The second sorcerer rushed at me and I saw him crumple as he approached. Corbel tore into him and punched through his chest, stopping him.

They weren't as distracted as I thought. I stood up and dusted myself off as Corbel stepped close.

"I thought you were immune to magic?" he said, coming close. "That air blast looked pretty effective as he knocked you on your ass."

"He didn't hit me with magic, he hit me with air that was affected by magic. Big difference."

"Means they know about you, so be ready for conventional attacks."

I nodded as we went up the stairs.

"If you see a red mist—" I started, but Corbel held up his hand as he pushed opened the door and looked in.

"You've survived chaotic mist?" he asked as he stepped inside.

I nodded. "One of these guys used it at the museum," I said. "Nasty stuff."

"You have no idea. Chaos is controlling these

sorcerers. It means he has their essence. We can't let him kill the last one—what's her name?"

"Roxanne. Does that mean he knows we're here?"

"He's known that the moment we stepped foot on the island," Corbel replied. "He picked this place so he can monitor who approaches. The entire island is runed."

"Shit, we need to find Monty."

"We need to split up. You look for Tristan, and I'll locate the sorceress," he said. "You see anyone who's not me or your friend—shoot first."

He headed up the monumental staircase that spiraled through the center of the tower. I walked forward and climbed another staircase.

The second level was empty. I arrived on the third level as the power shut off, casting the tower into darkness. I heard the whistling first and jumped down several steps as the staircase was peppered with what I thought were bullets.

I looked down and saw small chunks of concrete debris scattered across the stairs.

"Strong, you're too late," a voice said from the third level. "Your friends are gone."

"If that were true, you wouldn't be trying to give me a concrete makeover," I said. "Why don't you come out and face me?"

"Did you forget our last dance? You didn't do so well."

A figure moved behind me and I turned to shoot, when I saw it was Corbel with his hands up.

"Are you looking to get shot?" I said. "Stop being a ninja around me."

He snuck up the stairs and another barrage of projectiles smashed into the wall at the landing. I heard a scuffle and a muffled groan followed by a body rolling down the stairs. Another sorcerer. I bent over to check the body.

Corbel came down and stood next to me, keeping an eye on the stairwell.

"Nothing on the second level?" I asked.

"Nothing, Strong," he said, but his voice was off somehow.

It wasn't Corbel. I turned to fire as I sensed the rapid movement. A burning sensation exploded in my body as he shoved a knife into my side and jumped back. I fired twice. The first shot missed. The second shot slammed him against the wall as it punctured his chest.

"That looks like it hurts," Chaos said and laughed as the sorcerer dropped the illusion of Corbel and transformed back. "Just don't know who to trust these days." The entropy round winked him out of existence a second later.

I slowly pulled out the knife and saw the runes inscribed on the blade. The wound didn't close. I looked out one of the windows and saw the sun setting behind the New York City skyline. I was running out of time.

I climbed up the stairs to the third level and barely dodged a fireball that smashed into the wall next to me. I fired and caught the sorcerer in the leg as I stumbled back down the stairs. A few seconds later, he was gone. My vision tunneled in as I took a deep breath and steadied myself.

A figure came around the corner and I shot at it.

"Strong, if you shoot at me again I'm going to have to rip your arm off," Corbel said.

He looked around the corner again and I slumped against the wall as he approached.

"Last time I saw you, you buried a knife in my side," I said, showing him the wound. "I think it's poisoned. Blade was covered in runes."

"Clearly it wasn't me. Did you kill the sorcerer?" he asked as he pulled out a vial and poured it on the wound. The pain gripped my midsection and I nearly lost consciousness as a groan escaped my lips.

I nodded. "Are you trying to kill me and save Chaos the trouble?" I asked through clenched teeth.

"Try not to get stabbed again. I don't have any more of that," he said.

The effects of the poison began to wear off and I felt the wound close as my healing took over.

"What was that?" I said, looking at the closed wound. The skin around it was red, angry, and tender, but the wound was closed.

"Trust me, you don't want to know," he said, putting the vial away. "Aside from my twin, how many sorcerers have you faced?"

"Three inside the tower and the two outside."

"I dispatched two on my way here," he said. "By my calculations that leaves two sorcerers and Chaos. The other levels are clear. We have one more floor above us and the dome."

We headed up the flight of stairs. In the center of the floor lay a body with a blade buried in its abdomen, and my stomach dropped. It was Roxanne. I began approaching her, but Corbel held me back.

"She may still be alive," I said and pulled my arm away.

I crouched next to her and felt for a pulse. Corbel stood back, ready to attack if necessary. She was still alive, but barely. I grabbed the hilt, but she grabbed my hand.

"Don't, you'll spread the poison," she rasped. "I don't have long, Simon. You can't let Tristan do it. Don't let him give Chaos his blood."

"Can his blood save you?" I asked.

"He's a Golden Circle mage," Corbel said and crouched next to me. "With the right spell, it can heal her. Chaos will use that to get Tristan to agree."

I didn't notice the mist right away. By the time I turned to face the sorcerer, I realized we were in the middle of a cloud of chaotic mist. Corbel scooped up Roxanne as the second sorcerer came up the stairs behind us.

Corbel gestured behind me with his chin and I glanced over my shoulder. It was the stairway to the dome—and Chaos. I turned to run up the steps as Corbel pushed back and crashed into the sorcerer on the stairs.

I made it halfway up when I heard the familiar thump and was launched forward, sliding headfirst onto the next level.

"Bloody hell, Simon, you shouldn't have come," Monty said from across the floor. "That's what he was waiting for."

He was on his knees with his arms shackled to the floor. I could make out the silver restraints on his wrists and the runes on the chains. His head was slumped forward and his breathing was ragged.

"I told you, Tristan, the bonds of friendship are stronger than the ones holding you in place," Chaos said from the corner.

"Let him go," I said, aiming the Grim Whisper. "We took Roxanne and she's still alive. You failed. The ritual is over."

Chaos laughed and lifted his hand while making a gesture. Ten small white orbs materialized in front of him. Their light illuminated the dome.

"You're partially correct. The ritual is *almost* over. I just need one more thing from your friend Tristan."

"You shouldn't have come, Simon," Monty said, looking up at me. "Roxanne was a ploy. He has the essences."

The orbs raced across the floor and crashed into me faster than I could react. I felt the dome sway and I fell to my knees. I could sense Chaos walk over.

"I *had* the essences, Strong, and now you have them," he said, striking me across the face and turning my world black once again.

THIRTY-THREE

IT WAS STILL dark when I regained consciousness. My arms were shackled to the floor like Monty. The Ebonsoul and Grim Whisper lay in a corner next to the case holding the negation rune. I looked groggily around the room, but I didn't see Chaos.

My shirt and coat were gone and my chest burned. I looked down to see an angry red scar in the shape of the null rune traced on my chest.

"Simon, wake up," Monty said. "Focus—we don't have much time."

I pulled against the shackles but they wouldn't budge. My tongue was thick and my mouth felt full of cotton.

"Much time for what—until we die? These things aren't coming off and you're wearing restraints. I would say it's over."

"Not yet it isn't," he said, shaking his head. "You have to break the shackles."

"Let me check my pockets for a hacksaw. I'm pretty

sure I brought one," I said. "What do you want me to do—use magic?"

"Yes, you have the essence of ten sorcerers inside you," he said after a brief pause. "You need to activate the mala. Bring her here."

I looked down and saw the mala bracelet still around my wrist.

"Why didn't he remove it? It's not working."

"He tried and it prevented him, forcibly," he said. "Said he was going to come back and get that off. Its energy disrupts the ritual. You need to use it before he returns."

"How? It's not like I can reach it," I said, shaking my wrists. "Where did Chaos go?"

"Don't worry about that now. Focus, you don't need to touch it to make it work," he said. "Your chains aren't runed and he didn't put silver restraints on you."

"The mala *doesn't* work. I tried using it a few times and nothing happened. And I'm not you, Monty, I can't use magic."

"Simon, listen to me. Have you ever seen me hold a wand or staff?"

"No, you just kind of do your thing and demolish everything. Actually, now that I think of it, every time you've used magic something gets destroyed."

"I'm going to ignore that because it's clear you've suffered a blow to the head," he said. "Have you ever heard me use incantations or special words of power?"

"Are we counting all the times you curse?"

He gave me his 'don't be an idiot look,' and I knew it was the real Monty.

"A mage doesn't need a focus, like, say, a wizard or

sorcerer," he said. "A mage is both marble and chisel; magic flows in and through a mage."

"Sounds all warm and fuzzy, but that's not me, that's *you*."

"Everyone has the potential. Some more than others, but magic is available to anyone willing to tap into it," he said. "Right now those essences you are holding give you a distinct advantage. Activate the mala."

"How? I don't know *how*. It's not like it came with an instruction manual."

"Focus, the same way you were able to summon Karma to you the last time. Try and summon her again."

"That's not really motivating, you know," I said. "She wasn't exactly happy to be summoned."

"Chaos is going to return with etheric shears, which I believe is the only artifact that can cut through your mala without reducing this dome to dust," he said. "When he cuts your mala, the null rune on your chest will absorb the essence of the sorcerers inside your body and transform you into a vessel for the null rune. How's that for motivation?"

"Where's he getting these shears—Home Depot?"

"He can only get them in one place, which means he will need to steal them from the Fates."

"The Fates, as in the three ugly old ladies?" I asked. "The ones with one eye between them?"

"You're confusing the Fates with the Gray Sisters," he said. "Atropos holds the shears he needs, which means we have some time, but not much. They reside in Hades so he will have his hands full getting them."

"Could be that's why he exploded Hades' office," I

said. "Maybe he needs these shears for something else too?"

"You can ask him when he gets back—right now you need to activate the mala. Summon Karma."

I closed my eyes and took a few deep breaths to calm down. I didn't know if this was going to work, but it wasn't as if I had other options. I felt the energy inside me coalesce in my chest and get warmer.

"That's it, Simon, keep going," Monty said. "You're doing it."

"Not helping," I whispered as I tried to concentrate.

I focused on the warmth and it kept getting hotter until my chest burned. I opened my eyes and saw the null rune glowing. I swore I could smell burned flesh.

"Monty, this isn't working. All I'm doing is barbequing my chest. She isn't—" Then the room became hazy and out of focus. The smell of lotus flowers filled my nose.

"Hello, Simon," Karma said from behind me, her voice thick and husky. She stepped around to face me and I noticed she wasn't doing the college-student look this time. She was dressed in tight black leather that accentuated her curves. Her thigh-high boots glistened in the low light. All she needed was a whip to finish the dominatrix ensemble. I really hoped she was in a better mood this time.

"Hello, Karma," I said slowly. "I need help."

"You summoned me *again*?" she said and raised her hand. She stopped mid-swing and took in the scene. She narrowed her eyes and stared at me for a few seconds. The rune was no longer glowing, but I could still feel the burning radiating throughout my chest.

She lowered her arm and knelt in front of me. She traced the rune on my chest with a finger.

"Can you help us?" I asked. "Chaos is coming back any second with some shears and then it's all over."

She smiled. "Why? Is he giving you a haircut?"

"He's going to cut the mala and then the rune will destroy me," I said. "Can you at least release Monty?"

"The shears aren't for the mala, Simon, they're for you. Haven't you wondered how to kill an immortal?" she said. "He brings his own destruction."

"So you won't help?" I pleaded. "At least take off these shackles."

"No, I won't help you," she said, her voice hard. "Because you don't need it. Use the tools you have in hand."

She gently patted my cheek, which only felt like a five-pound hammer this time as my head rocked to the side.

"I don't know what you mean," I said in confusion as I raised my hand to rub my face. Her leather creaked as she stood in front of me. I looked down at my arms, which were no longer being held by shackles. "You?"

She pointed at me and shook her head. "You," she said. "He's coming back. Free your friend and prepare. If you survive this, I would like to know how you summoned me this time."

She disappeared as the room snapped back into focus and I ran over to Monty. I touched the silver restraints and they fell off to the side. I shoved them away with my foot.

"Step back," he said. "I have to get these off."

The shackles grew white hot as they melted away

from him. That was when I heard the soft clapping behind us.

"You two have certainly made this interesting. I'm really going to miss you both."

Chaos stepped forward, holding a large sword.

"Whatever you do, don't let that sword cut you," Monty whispered. "That's Atropos's shears. It can and will kill you."

"Shears means scissors in this country, Monty, not a sword," I whispered back, my eyes focused on the weapon.

Chaos hefted the sword in front of him as if testing its balance. "Much better than a pair of scissors, don't you think?"

"I think you should return that to where you got it, that's what I think," I answered as I backed up.

"Time to die," he said and lunged forward.

THIRTY-FOUR

I JUMPED INTO the corner and grabbed my weapons as Chaos clenched his hand into a fist and the rune on my chest exploded with light.

"Simon!" Monty yelled.

I fell forward as Monty launched two black orbs from his hands at Chaos. Monty threw my coat over me and the pain in my chest subsided. Chaos sliced through the orbs, resulting in an explosion that sent him through the wall of the tower as it collapsed in a mound of debris.

"What the—?" I said and gasped, trying to catch my breath.

"The essences. You aren't immune to magic while those things are inside of you. Close the coat. The runes should help."

"Negation rune," I managed as I stood slowly and pointed. "In the case."

"If I unleash it in here it will undo us all," he said as he grabbed the case and pulled out the rune.

"If you don't, he gets the null rune. No choice."

"I can't throw it at him—it needs to touch him."

"I know," I said. "Activate it and set it to go off in ten seconds. I'll make sure it touches him."

"Simon—" he started.

"No need to say it, Monty. Besides in the words of the great Freddy Mercury, who wants to live forever?"

He activated the rune and I placed it around my neck and ran for the hole filled with debris. Chaos charged at me and I activated my mark. Everything went out of focus.

"That won't save you," Chaos said as he closed on me.

"I know," I said with a grunt as he ran me through with the shears. "I'm not looking to be saved."

I drew Grim Whisper and fired several shots into his chest. He laughed in my face.

"I told you runed rounds were ineffective," he said. "You just don't have the firepower, Strong. You should have joined me. Your entire existence is chaos and yet you refute me. Now you're going to die here."

"You're just like me," I said. "In this space we are the same. You aren't immortal."

"You think a few bullets can end me?" he said, stepping close.

Nothing happened for a few seconds and then I saw the whirlwinds begin to form. It was my turn to smile.

"Those weren't runed rounds," I whispered as he grabbed me by the throat. I grabbed the negation rune from around my neck and touched it to his arm, watching as it exploded in light.

His scream filled my ears as he let me go. I fell to my

knees as the entropy rounds began to work on him and the small whirlwinds joined to form one large one.

"You can't kill chaos," he said. "I am infinite. I am entropy. I am everlasting."

"I may not be able to kill you, but I can sure as hell stop you from destroying everything and starting another war."

"Your naiveté will be your undoing. Another war is inevitable," he said. "It is the only way. Eventually everything must fall to entropy."

"You know what? Take some entropy—to go," I said.

I fired one last time, putting a round in his forehead.

"You can't kill me. I'm Chaos!" The whirlwinds engulfed him and he disappeared.

The sword fell next to me on the floor and reverted to a large pair of rune-covered shears. The world snapped back into focus and I felt the cool night breeze on my skin. Most of the dome lay in ruins. I looked up into the night sky as the stars winked back at me. I fell on my side, hearing footsteps approach. Monty's concerned face came into my field of vision.

"You did it, Simon," he said as he removed the negation rune from my neck. "You stopped him."

"*We* stopped him. Entropy rounds for the win," I said as I grabbed his arm.

"Lay still, help is on the way," he said. "Stop talking for once."

"You look like crap. I mean more than usual."

He said something, but the whirring of helicopter blades drowned out his response. I felt myself being lifted and then everything fell away.

THIRTY-FIVE

THE DELICATE SOUND of china gently colliding filled my ears. I kept my eyes closed and the smell of Earl Grey filled my nose.

"It's certainly about time," Monty said, placing the cup on the side table. "Do you intend to laze about indefinitely?"

"This must be the part where the nightmare begins," I mumbled as I tried to sit up. A pair of strong hands held me down and I looked up into Roxanne's face.

"Not quite time for you to be moving about," she said with a smile. "You need rest."

"You look well," I said, and she looked over her shoulder at Monty.

"His doing," she said. "He found me after you stopped Chaos."

I looked at Monty and I swear he blushed.

"It wasn't much," Monty said with a cough. "I mean, Corbel did much of the work, much to my surprise."

"You saved my life," Roxanne said. "Thank you."

"Corbel made it?" I asked. "Is Hades back?"

"No sign of Hades or Corbel after that night," Monty answered, picking up the cup and taking a sip. "But I'm sure they will turn up, eventually."

"How long have I been here?" I asked.

"Five days in and out of consciousness." She looked at me while picking up a clipboard. "You should be able to be discharged tomorrow."

"Just as well," Monty said. "He has a creature to tend to."

"Try not to tax him, Tristan, he needs his rest," she said as she put the clipboard back and headed to the door. "I'll be back to check on you later, Simon."

Monty nodded and walked her to the door. He said something to her I couldn't make out. She smiled and nodded. He came back to sit next to me after she left.

"You dog, you finally asked her out?" I said, chuckling.

"No, I merely pointed out that you haven't been having regular bowel movements and that she should start enema treatments thrice daily," he said with a straight face. "Wouldn't want your system to get backed up.

"Shit," I said with a groan as I shifted my weight. "That's not funny."

"Precisely," he answered. "Poor bowel movements can be a serious issue."

"Hilarious. You should take your show on the road," I said as he cracked a smile. "Any sign of Chaos?"

He grew serious and shook his head. "Once Hades returns, we should have a conversation with him. It seems Charon is back on duty and he expresses thanks for his release."

"What happened to Ramirez?" I asked. "I left him in front of the detention center."

"Uncovering that black site got him fired as a lieutenant…" Monty said.

"Damn, maybe there's someone we can call."

"…And promoted to Director of the NYTF. Seems there was some corruption connected to the detention center and the NYTF. He's been tasked with eliminating it."

"Good for him, he deserves it," I said, relieved. "Now he can afford to buy me dinner. Did you check on Allen?"

"Full recovery and use of his arm with a little help from Roxanne. He'll be examining strange corpses for the foreseeable future."

I nodded and sighed. "Thanks, he's good people."

He stood and brushed off his suit and looked at his watch.

"Nice suit. Roselli's?" I asked.

He nodded. "Your vampire requested my presence in your absence. They will be designating a downtown location neutral territory and I'm told this is your doing," he said.

I nodded. "Jimmy the Cleaver. He's the new butcher in the meat market and a Werebear from up north."

"Jimmy the Cleaver—I'm sure he's charming," he said and straightened the sleeves of his jacket.

"Has Michiko—?"

"She's been here every night since you arrived and no doubt will be here again tonight at some point."

I smiled at that. I looked forward to seeing her,

scowl and all.

"However, I'm happy to report that the office has been vampire-free since the creature arrived."

"Peaches—his name is Peaches."

"I refuse to address him as a fruit," he said. "Change the name."

He turned and headed to the door.

"Hey, Monty…" I said, serious.

"Yes," he said and stopped without turning around.

"Just wanted to say thanks. I couldn't have done it without you," I said. "You're more than my friend, you're my family."

His back stiffened a bit and he grabbed the handle, opening the door.

"Being family means never having to say thanks, Simon," he whispered, pulling the door open. "I'll see you in the morning."

He walked out of the room and the door clicked shut.

THIRTY-SIX

"HELLO, SIMON," THE voice whispered. "How is my splinter feeling?"

Michiko had left about half an hour earlier. She came by to inform me that Yama and Georgianna would be staying with Monty and me indefinitely. It wasn't a request. I knew it was an excuse, because she stayed for another hour afterward. This meant I was wide-awake for my new visitor.

"Hello, Karma," I said and noticed that everything was still in focus. She wasn't warping time with this visit. "I'm sore pretty much everywhere."

She was dressed in a nurse's uniform, picked up my clipboard, and sat in the chair next to the bed.

"Looks like you'll be leaving here soon," she said. "I still need something from you, though."

"We didn't kill him, did we?" I asked, knowing the answer but wanting her to confirm it.

She gave me a quick smile and short shake of her head.

"Entropy rounds—clever and ironic. Where did you get them?"

I saw no point in lying. Besides, she probably knew the truth.

"Monty," I said. "He made them."

"They have been banned from use for over a century," she said. "Energy like that doesn't go unnoticed."

"What're you trying to say?"

"You're growing in power and even used magic."

"That was unintentional," I said, "and Monty's fault."

She laughed and the room grew a few degrees cooler.

"Ah, my guest is here. Please lay still."

She gestured with her hands. It reminded me of something Monty had done a few days earlier. I felt warmth in my abdomen and ten small orbs floated up from my chest. A figure appeared behind her.

"Hello, Simon," he said. "It is good to see you whole."

"Charon. I heard you were back on duty."

The orbs floated away from me and vanished into his hand.

"Thank you," he said and bowed. "The balance must always be restored."

"No offense, but I don't plan on seeing you anytime soon," I said.

"None taken. I suspect it will be quite some time before I have to escort you, Simon."

He gave me a short nod and disappeared. The temperature in the room increased instantly.

"You and Tristan have made some powerful allies and even more powerful enemies," she said once Charon had disappeared.

"That sounds like I should retire. As far as enemies, Chaos was pretty bad," I said. "If we didn't kill him, what did we do—send him on vacation?"

"You did what some considered impossible. You destroyed his corporeal form. Granted you had help, but it is an impressive feat."

"How soon before he comes back?"

I had this image of a pissed-off Chaos showing up at my front door and shredding it and me while I stood there in my underwear.

"About a century, give or take a decade. Plenty of time to prepare."

"Prepare? Prepare for what?"

"There are others you need to focus on. Some bent on starting another war, and some just hungry for power. You will need to confront both."

"Me? Isn't that what the Dark Council is for?"

She smiled and patted me on the cheek without rattling teeth from my head. "Some of them are *part* of the Dark Council. Chaos spoke truth—war is inevitable. We can deny it or prepare for it."

"That is an outcome I would prefer avoiding, if possible."

"It's not. It will be increasingly difficult for you and Tristan to remain obscure. Once Hades returns, he'll want to see you."

"Can't say I'm looking forward to that," I said. "I can't help feeling he has some kind of agenda."

"There is a saying: 'You can always judge a man by

the loyalty of his friends and the quality of his enemies.' You and Tristan have made a great deal of both."

"That's good. Who said it?"

She stood, returned the clipboard to its holder, and smiled at me.

"I did—just now."

"I thought that was Oscar Wilde."

"And where do you think *he* heard it? I *will* see you soon, Simon."

She vanished, leaving me in the room alone with my thoughts. The sun was hinting at rising as the clouds turned pink on the horizon. It was going to be a good day.

THE END

CAST OF CHARACTERS FOR

TOMBYARDS & BUTTERFLIES

ALLEN MONTGOMERY-MEDICAL Examiner for the NYTF. Specializes in supernatural autopsies. Liaison for the OCME and the NYTF. If Allen hasn't seen it, it doesn't exist.

Andrei Belyakov-Olga's eyes and ears at The Moscow. He handles the day-to-day affairs of the building and reports to Olga.

Angel Ramirez-Lieutenant of the NYTF and friend to Simon Strong. Cannot believe how much destruction one detective agency can wage in the course of one day.

Cecil Fairchild-Owner of SuNaTran and close friend of Tristan Montague. Provides transport for the supernatural community and has been known to make a vehicle disappear in record time.

Chaos-(AKA the chasm, the gap) Entropy

personified. The ultimate undoing of order and balance in the universe. Wants to end it-ALL. Known to crash parties and events bringing them to a swift end.

Charon-(AKA The Ferryman) carries the souls of the newly deceased across the river Styx into the Underworld. Most senior of the psychopomps, occasionally given special projects to fulfill. Would really prefer a week off-with pay.

Corbel Nwobon-(AKA the 'Hound of Hades') Enforcer of the Underworld. Occasionally smells of fire and brimstone from frequent visits to the Underworld.

Ezrael-(AKA Ezra, Azrael-the Angel of Death, Death, Thanatos, Big D) the personification of Death. Feared, disliked, and respected by human and supernatural alike. Loves pastrami on rye and sitting in his favorite deli on 1st Avenue studying when he isn't out "collecting" or in his office at Arkangel Industries.

Georgianna Wittenbraden-Vampire of a powerful clan who is currently shunned and being assisted by the Montague & Strong Detective Agency.

The Hack-Cybercriminal, security expert, and friend of Simon. He is feared and hunted by every three-letter agency on the planet. If it's digital it's at risk.

Hades-Ruler of the Underworld. Rules the dead and is generally seen around funerals and wakes. Favorite song by the Eagles is 'Hotel California'-especially that part about checking out, but never leaving.

Ken Nakatomi-Michiko's brother and elite assassin for the Dark Council. If you're his target and you see him-it's the last thing you ever see.

Kali-(AKA Divine Mother) goddess of Time, Creation, Destruction, and Power. Cursed Simon for unspecified reasons and has been known to hold a grudge. She is also one of the most powerful magic-users in existence.

Karma-The personification of causality, order, and balance. She reaps what you sow. Also known as the mistress of bad timing. Everyone knows the saying karma is a…some days that saying is true.

Michiko Nakatomi-(AKA 'Chi' if you've grown tired of breathing) Vampire leader of the Dark Council. Reputed to be the most powerful vampire in the Council.

Noh Fan Yat- Martial arts instructor for the Montague & Strong Detective Agency. Teacher to both Simon and Tristan. Known for his bamboo staff of pain and correction.

Olga Etrechenko-Simon's landlord and current owner of The Moscow. She has an uncanny ability for tracking Simon down when the rent is due. You never cheat Olga.

Peaches-(AKA Devildog, Hellhound, Arm Shredder and Destroyer of Limbs) Offspring of Cerberus and given to the Montague & Strong Detective Agency to help with their security. Closely resembles a Cane Corso.

Piero Roselli-Vampire and owner of Roselli's-an upscale restaurant and club that caters to the supernatural community. If Piero doesn't seat you, you aren't staying.

Robert Bellamy-Driver for SuNaTran and Cecil

Fairchild. Formality is non-negotiable.

Roxanne DeMarco-Director of Haven. Oversees both the Medical and Detention Centers of the facility. Is an accomplished sorceress with formidable skill. Has been known to make Tristan stammer and stutter with merely a touch of his arm.

Simon Strong-The intelligent (and dashingly handsome) half of the Montague & Strong Detective Agency. Cursed alive into immortality by the goddess Kali.

Tristan Montague- The civilized (and staggeringly brilliant) half of the Montague & Strong Detective Agency. Mage of the Golden Circle sect and currently on 'extended leave' from their ever-watchful supervision.

Yama-Assigned bodyguard to Georgianna. A personal guard of Michiko Nakatomi. He is known to exhibit dizzying heights of eloquence in grunts and stares.

ORGANIZATIONS

CHRISTYE, BLAHQ, &DOIL-Law firm that shares the same floor with the Montague & Strong Detective Agency. Never seem to be open, but always ready for business.

New York Task Force-(AKA the NYTF) a quasi-military police force created to deal with any supernatural event occurring in New York City.

SuNaTran-(AKA Supernatural Transportations) Owned by Cecil Fairchild. Provides car and vehicle service to the supernatural community in addition to magic-users who can afford membership.

The Dark Council- Created to maintain the peace between humanity and the supernatural community shortly after the last Supernatural War. Its role is to be a check and balance against another war occurring. Not everyone in the Council favors peace.

AUTHOR NOTES

I WANT TO thank you for reading this story and joining me in this adventure. If you've read some of my other books, you will notice that while this book is filled with action it also contains generous amounts of humor and even hints at (gasp) romance.

This book was my way of taking a chance on trying something different and new (for me). I really enjoyed discovering about Monty & Strong and their assorted cast of friends (and enemies). Writing this story for you was an absolute blast.

If you enjoyed it and would like to see more of Monty & Strong-**please do me a HUGE favor and leave a review.** It's really important and helps the book (and me). Plus it means Peaches gets more chew toys to shred and we want to keep Peaches happy, don't we?

I really appreciate your feedback. Let me know what you thought by emailing me at www.orlando@orlandoasanchez.com or join the Facebook group titled Montague & Strong Case Files.

You can also find my other books at:
www.orlandoasanchez.com

You can follow Monty & Strong on twitter where they exchange ideas and quips and usually disagree about everything: Tristan can be followed here @MageMontague and Simon can be followed here @MontyandStrong.

I also wanted to give you something a little extra for getting my book. Included is the first chapter of the next Montague & Strong story here for you to read. Enjoy!

FULL MOON HOWL

A MONTAGUE AND Strong Detective Novel

ONE

"SHE TOLD ME you could help me. I need to stop this tonight—before the change," he pleaded as he gripped the edge of the conference table. "Before I hurt someone else."

I opened my mouth to speak and immediately regretted it. The stench wafting across the table sucker-punched me, forcing me to grimace as I held my breath. The smell hung on him—a shroud of illness that filled the room. Part of me wished Charon would stroll through the door or wall any second and claim him just to clear the air.

The other part realized we were dealing with a real threat. A sick Were was a dangerous Were. The snuffling and rumbling from under the table told me Peaches was having a hard time breathing too. Only Monty seemed immune to the putrid miasma crawling across the room. If he smelled anything, his sense of propriety would never let him outwardly display it. He was English, after all.

Douglas Bishop, our Were client, was a nervous, thin man of medium height. His pale skin glistened in the waning rays of sunlight that crept through the window.

A worn gray suit a few sizes too large draped itself over his body. He completed the ensemble with a sweat-stained off-white shirt and dark tie. His hands let go of the conference table and were clasped tightly before him. He would clench them into fists after every sentence, followed by pushing his glasses up the bridge of his nose. Yes, it was driving me crazy. A pair of silver restraints sat on the table next to him. I had silver ammo in the Grim Whisper, and Monty as backup. Better to have it and not need it than the alternative.

"You have to do this—before the change," he pleaded again. "You have to reverse this."

"Lycanthropy is irreversible. It can't be undone," Monty said, flexing his fingers. "Weren't you informed of this?"

"Then kill me before I hurt someone else," Douglas said. "Please." His body seized and he coughed uncontrollably. It was a wet sound that went on for nearly half a minute.

"Do you want some water?" I asked, but he waved me away and managed to get himself under control.

"We have plenty of pests in this office, but we are not an extermination service," Monty said, his voice hard as he looked at me.

"You have to help me," Douglas said and shivered. "I can't go out. I'm not safe—no one is safe."

"When did you first realize you were ill?" I asked through shallow breaths. "How long have you been like this?"

"Since the last full moon," he said and coughed again, hacking a glob of phlegm onto the conference table.

My stomach clenched and I resisted the urge to revisit my lunch.

"I'm sorry," Douglas said and wiped the phlegm with his sleeve, smearing it across the table. "I can't control it."

"This is what we get for listening to that vampire of yours," Monty muttered as he stood to get disinfectant and a cloth to wipe down the table.

"If Chi sent him, it was important," I said, taking my hands off the table. "What do you mean before the change? It's not a full moon tonight."

"Doesn't matter. I've been changing every night since I felt like this," Douglas said. "Don't need a moon."

"You're changing without a full moon? Only very old and powerful Were can do that," Monty answered, cleaning the table. "And you're neither. This may have a deeper source. I don't think it's some Were infection."

"Douglas, have you tried going to the Dark Council?" I asked. "They really are equipped to deal with this sort of thing."

"The Dark Council told me they couldn't help me!" he yelled, pounding the table. "They said it was hopeless and that I should just end it or have someone do it for me."

A low rumble crept along the floor from under the table.

"Douglas, I need you to calm down," I said, glancing at Peaches. "And I mean now."

He took a deep breath and sat back in his chair. I looked under the table again. Peaches was no longer sprawled but rested on his stomach and focused on Douglas. He gave me a quick look as if to say 'can I have him for lunch?' I shook my head and he dropped his head, clearly disappointed.

"Sometimes the body can't resist the turning and it has an adverse reaction," Monty said, moving to the other side of the table. "Although I haven't seen anything this severe. Have you been exposed to any strange magic?"

"You don't understand," Douglas said, and I saw him convulse. "I can't control it. Once I turn, I'm a threat, a menace to anyone around me."

"I get it, and right now turning is not a good idea," I said, pushing my chair back. "Let's think some calm thoughts and see if we can solve this."

"It's too late, it's happening," he said and clenched his teeth as he gripped the table. "You need to run. Get away while you can."

I reached for the silver restraints that were on the table and attempted to put them on his wrists. I managed to get one on him and I received a hairy back-fist in return. I slid down the conference table and over the end.

I got to my feet and saw Douglas convulse again as his body shifted and began the transformation. The restraint had no effect. He shredded his oversized suit and went full werewolf.

"Monty, the restraint isn't stopping the turn. Are you sure it isn't a full moon?" I asked. "You didn't schedule to meet a sick Were during a full moon, did you,

Monty?"

"No," Monty answered as he stepped back. "I wouldn't have scheduled this meeting on a full moon, Simon. This is a forced change and looks like dark magic."

"Well, *he* didn't get the memo," I said, pointing at Douglas as he turned. "What do you mean dark magic? He's a werewolf not a sorcerer."

I didn't want to shoot Douglas. He seemed like a nice person and had come to us for help. The werewolf he transformed into, however—not so nice.

The smell intensified with the transformation, which I didn't think was possible. It was now an essence of wet dog with a side of vomit. His bloodshot eyes fixed on me and he snarled. Peaches answered with a growl of his own.

"Hello, Tristan," Werewolf Douglas rasped. "It really has been too long."

"It's for you," I said as I moved back. "You know him?"

"I've never met him before today. Who sent you?" Monty asked Douglas.

"Looks like he knows you." I shrugged.

"Oh, I do," Douglas said with a snarl. "I'm coming and I'm bringing hell with me, Tristan."

"Much better in *Tombstone* when Kurt Russell said it," I answered. "Why don't you de-wolf and we can speak like civilized creatures?"

"I have a message for you, mage," Douglas said and raked a claw across the conference table—the very expensive mahogany conference table. Monty clenched his jaw, flexed his hands, and narrowed his eyes as he looked down at the marks.

I looked down and saw that the claw marks were a design. It reminded me of crude Nazca lines. This one looked like a bird with wings outstretched.

"Whom shall I say is delivering this message?" Monty asked, his voice grim. "Do you have a name?"

"I'm going to start with the Weres first and then I'm going to erase all of the abominations," Douglas rasped and coughed up more phlegm. "I'll leave you and the golden mages for last, old friend."

"I have a message for you, Doug—bath… posthaste," I said, trying to breathe through my mouth and not gag. "Seriously, the reekage is strong with this one, Monty."

"Do I know you?" Monty asked as Peaches bounded out from under the table and lunged at Douglas. He backhanded Peaches across the room, which only made him angry as he stalked back. Peaches, an offspring of Cerberus, was not your average hound.

Douglas jumped over the table and landed next to me. He raked his claws across my chest and got my attention in a hurry. Monty hit him with an orb of air, which punched into his chest and turned him around. He recovered fast enough to impale my arm with his other hand. He pulled me close and nearly knocked me unconscious with his breath.

"Douglas, would a breath mint be asking too much —ahh—?" I said as he squeezed his claws into my arm and pulled my face close to his. His bloodshot eyes gazed into mine as drool escaped the side of his mouth.

"Behold, I am coming quickly and my reward is with

me. To give to each according to what he has done. I am the Alpha and the Omega, the First and the Last, the Beginning and the End," he said and tossed me across the room.

I managed to twist my body midair and caught a glimpse of him closing on me. I pulled out Grim Whisper and fired twice as I landed on my back. The rounds hit him square in the chest. The effect was immediate. He transformed back into human form and died several seconds later.

"Shit, Monty," I said, angry. "I didn't want to kill him. The restraint didn't work. Why didn't it work?"

"I don't know," Monty whispered, and removed the restraint, inspecting it. "These restraints are designed to negate a Were turning. I've never seen them fail."

"I had to shoot him," I said. "He didn't look like he was getting closer to chatting."

The claw marks on my chest and arm burned and itched as they started to heal. My immunity to magic extended to vampires trying to drain me and werewolves intent on removing parts of my body. Still hurt like hell, though. I looked down at my ruined shirt and cursed.

"This was a Balmain, Monty," I said, pointing at my shirt. "I'm out a shirt thanks to a psycho werewolf."

"He was unwell," Monty answered, pensive.

"Is that what you're calling unwell?" I said. "He was *infected*. Like the other Were we chased down in the Village."

"I'm more concerned about the messages. That pattern of speech sounded familiar."

"If the restraint had worked, we could ask him," I

said, looking at Douglas's lifeless body. "I'd better call Allen. A dead Were is bad news."

"You had no choice, but you will have to explain this to the Dark Council, and your vampire."

"I know. I don't think she'll be pleased. The last part, that quote—the one he recited, I've heard it before," I said. "Sounded biblical."

"Revelation 22:12, 13," Monty said rubbing his chin. "Speaks of the second coming of Christ according to the Bible."

"Douglas was being controlled by the Christian messiah?" I said, shaking my head. "Somehow I doubt that."

"I don't recall ever reading where he is a werewolf," Monty replied. "At least not in *my* studies."

"Then that means someone who can turn a werewolf without a full moon is coming to pay us a visit."

"Sounds like an impending catastrophe," Monty answered and made his way to the kitchen.

"Is there another kind?" I asked, holstering Grim Whisper and pulling out my phone.

"No," he said. "I'd better make some tea."

Coming June 2017

Thank You!

If you enjoyed this book, would you please help me by leaving a review? It only needs to be a sentence or two and it would really help me out a lot!

Leave a review on Amazon US
Leave a review on Amazon UK

Get FREE stories here!

www.OrlandoASanchez.com
Free stories denoted below with an asterisk

All of My Books

*Books denoted with an asterisk are only available via my website!

The Warriors of the Way
The Karashihan* • Spiritual Warriors • The Ascendants • The Fallen Warrior • The Warrior Ascendant • The Master Warrior

John Kane
The Deepest Cut* • Blur

Sepia Blue
The Last Dance* • Rise of the Night

Chronicles of the Modern Mystics
A Dark Flame • A Dream of Ashes

Montague & Strong Detective Agency
Tombyards & Butterflies

Get them on Amazon

Amazon US
Amazon UK

ACKNOWLEDGMENTS

I'm finally beginning to understand that each book, each creative expression usually has a large group of people behind it. This book is no different. So let me take a moment to acknowledge my (very large) group:

To Dolly: my wife and biggest fan. You make all of this possible and keep me grounded, especially when I get into my writing to the exclusion of everything else. Thank you, I love you.

To my Tribe: You are the reason I have stories to tell. You cannot possibly fathom how much and how deep I love you all.

To Lee: Because you were the first audience I ever had. I love you sis.

To the Logsdon family: JL you saw the script and pushed me to bring my A-game and flesh it out into a story. LL your notes and comments turned this story from good to great.

Your patience knows no bounds. Thank you both.

Arigatogozaimasu

<u>To my Launch Team</u>: Dolly S. Steve L. Bill T. Mark R. Leslie P. Tracy B.

MaryAnn S. Chris S. Jonathan G. Penny C-M. Derek C. Tammy B. Angie H. Kate. John P L.(Author Guru Extraordinaire) Rachel S. Darren. David S.

Bryan G. Michelle S. Kerry. Brian R. Melissa K. Katy L. Jim Z. Marie McC. Jeff B. Carrie O'L. Bill H. Carmen E. Leigh Ann M. Channah H.(Blurb Jedi). Chris P. Cheryl. Cassandra H. Myles C. Terry B. Lorella. Lawrence G. Wayne G. P Sophie.

ART-Advance Reader Team

(In no particular order)

EricCandace, Carrie, Thomas, Brenda,

Timothy,Frederick,Cassandra,Penny,Tracy,
Maryann,Bill,Isabel,Elena,Mae,

Christopher,Stephanie,Joscelyn,Marie,Darre
n.

You took on reading my (very) rough draft
and helped me polish it into something
resembling a legible book. YOU GUYS
ROCK!

The Montague & Strong Case Files Group-(We need a shorter name.)

Dolly,Danetta,Darren,Thomas,Joscelyn,Isa
bel,Stephanie,Marie,Maryann,

Orlando(the younger),Mark,Myles Mary,Bill
T,EricCandace,Timothy,Michelle,Steve,

Jim,David,Tami,Kevin,Rita,Amy,

Sherrie,Daniel,Melissa,Mel,Chris,Brian,Der
ek,Elena,Aaron,Jeff, Bill H.,Carrie
Angela,Christopher,Channah,Larry,Brenda,
Cassandra,Laird Bruce,Tracy,
Jonathan,Penny,Mae,Charles,John,Fleur,Da
n,Paul,JC,Tom,

Melissa, Annie.

You all withstood the torture of
snippets(lol) and shared your insights into
the characters, the story and other
ideas(looking at you, Jim) that sometimes
my brain was not caffeinated enough for.
Thank you for being part of this group and
M&S. You each made it possible. Also one
of you needs to come up with a shorter
name for our mob.

TEA-The English Advisory

(they needed a posh name, being

English and all)

Aaron, Penny, Carrie

This small but select group advised me on all things English. Since I wasn't born in the UK they helped with ideas regarding Monty's speech and behavior. If Monty seems to be authentically English it's due to this group…Cheers!

WTA-The Incorrigibles

JL,BenZ, EricQK,and S.S.

They sound like a bunch of badass misfits because they are. Thank you for helping(corrupting) me into getting this book done. My exposure to the slightly deranged and extremely deviant brain trust that you are made this book possible. I humbly thank you.

<u>Deranged Doctor Design</u>

Kim, Darja, and Milo

You define professionalism and creativity.
Thank you for the great service and
amazing covers!

<u>To you the reader</u>:

Thank you for getting on this ride with me.
I truly hope you enjoy this story. You are
the reason I wrote it.

ABOUT THE AUTHOR

Orlando Sanchez has been writing ever since his teens when he was immersed in creating scenarios for playing Dungeon and Dragons with his friends every weekend. An avid reader, his influences are too numerous to list here. Some of the most prominent are: J.R.R. Tolkien, Jim Butcher, Kat Richardson, Terry Pratchett, Terry Brooks, Christopher Moore, Piers Anthony, Lee Child, George Lucas, Andrew Vachss, and Barry Eisler to name a few in no particular order.

The worlds of his books are urban settings with a twist of the paranormal lurking just behind the scenes and generous doses of magic, martial arts, mayhem, and mischief.

Aside from writing, he holds a 2nd and 3rd Dan in two distinct styles of Karate. If not training, he is studying some aspect of the martial arts or martial arts philosophy.

He currently resides in Queens, NY with his wife and children and can often be found in the local Starbucks where most of his writing is done.

Please visit his site at OrlandoASanchez.com for more information about his books and upcoming releases.

Copyright © 2017 by Orlando A. Sanchez

Published by OM Publishing NY NY

Cover Design by Deranged Doctor Design
www.derangeddoctordesign.com

18359143R00186

Printed in Poland
by Amazon Fulfillment
Poland Sp. z o.o., Wrocław